Secret Clues
The Mystery Club 1

Fiona Kelly

KNIGHT BOOKS
Hodder and Stoughton

580755
JCY

The characters and situations in this book are entirely imaginary and bear no relation to any real person or actual happenings.

The right of Fiona Kelly to be identified as the author of this work has been asserted by her in accordance with the Copyright, Designs and Patents Act 1988.

Printed and bound in Great Britain for Hodder and Stoughton Children's Books, a division of Hodder and Stoughton Ltd, Mill Road, Dunton Green, Sevenoaks, Kent TN13 2YA (Editorial Office: 47 Bedford Square, London WC1B 3DP) by Cox & Wyman Ltd, Reading, Berks. Typeset by Hewer Text Composition Services, Edinburgh.

A Catalogue record for this book is available from the British Library

ISBN 0 340 58867 5

To Francine Pascal, with thanks

1   Enemies and friends

'If you're not back in ten minutes, I'm going on
without you. I mean it, Jamie.' Holly Adams sat
on the bench in the old churchyard, watching her
younger brother as he ran back to the computer
games shop.

They were out exploring the town. At least,
Holly was trying to explore. Jamie seemed more
interested in spending his pocket money as rapidly as possible. *Eleven year old boys are like that*,
thought Holly, her intelligent grey eyes taking in
her surroundings. Holly was fifteen.

Behind her the church reared up into the blue
sky. Bright sunlight dappled the grass through tall
rhododendron bushes.

This is a lovely place, thought Holly, tucking her
long brown hair behind her ears. *So peaceful*.

She and her family had been living in the
small Yorkshire town of Willow Dale for only a
week, and Holly, with her naturally outgoing and
inquisitive nature, wanted to take everything in.
After all, this new setting, nestled in amongst the
rolling green Yorkshire hills, was going to be her

7

home from now on, and Holly was determined to make the best of things.

A few feet away from her, beyond the corner of the church, was a narrow alley-way bounded by black railings.

It was from this alley, out of sight but well within earshot, that she heard the two voices.

'Well, Harry, I'm back,' she heard one man say. 'We've got a bit of unfinished business, you and me. I kept my mouth shut because you told me the money would be waiting for me when I got out,' said the voice. 'Well, I'm out. And I want my money.'

'You'll get your money, Barney,' the other man said in a low, harsh voice. 'Don't you worry. There's a lad owes me money. You call in the debt and it's yours.' A snarl of laughter sounded. 'I don't suppose you'll have much trouble getting the money off him. He's just a kid who's got himself in over his head.'

'I'd better not,' said the first man. 'Because if I do, I'll be straight back to you. And next time I won't be in the mood for a chat. Got me?'

'Trust me, Barney. Put a bit of pressure on the lad and he'll pay up. Don't you worry.'

Barney laughed gratingly. 'I'm not worried, Harry.'

Holly glanced round and saw the back of a thin man as he walked rapidly away from her. He was wearing a tatty old leather jacket with a flying eagle printed on the back.

Holly shivered. Perhaps Willow Dale wasn't as peaceful as she had imagined.

A heavy set, hard-faced man emerged from the alley, wearing a suit. He had slicked-down dark hair and a small moustache. He adjusted his tie and seemed about to walk off in the opposite direction when he caught sight of Holly.

His eyes narrowed. Holly quickly looked away.

She felt his eyes boring into her for a second or two, then heard the crunch of gravel as he walked away.

Holly wished she hadn't heard the exchange between the two men. There had been something brutal in the voices. Holly didn't want to stay in the churchyard any more. She stood up and made her way back to the main street to find her brother.

Jamie was deep in computer games. Holly virtually had to drag him out of the shop.

'They've got all the latest stuff,' Jamie told her as they continued their exploration of the town.

'Dad told you they would have, didn't he?' said Holly.

Jamie shrugged. 'I suppose so,' he said. He looked round at her. 'I'm hungry,' he said. 'Let's get something to eat.'

They found a hamburger bar. The rest of Willow

Dale would have to wait. After all, they had plenty of time to explore their new home.

Holly sat enthralled as Mr Barnard strode back and forth across the front of the class. This was her first art lesson at her new school and she was determined to make a good impression.

Mr Barnard was telling them about oil painting.

'This school is full of old paintings,' he told them. 'I strongly advise you to spend some time having a good look at them.'

'Are we going to be doing any oil painting, sir?' asked a boy at the front.

'Not unless we suddenly come into a lot of money,' said Mr Barnard, with the grin that Holly was already liking. 'Oils cost a fortune. You'll have to make do with poster paint, I'm afraid.'

'We could buy some with the cash left over after we've finished collecting for the new gym, sir,' said someone else.

Mr Barnard laughed. 'I shouldn't be too hopeful about that, Andy,' he said. 'At the rate it's been going we shan't be able to afford that for the next twenty years, never mind having any money left over.'

The bell sounded for the end of the lesson. There was a general scraping of chair legs.

'For homework I want each of you to choose a painting in the school,' Mr Barnard shouted above the noise. 'Write me three hundred words on why you like it. OK? Class dismissed.'

10

Holly hung back as the others made the usual rush for the door.

'Ah! The new girl. Holly Adams, isn't it?' said Mr Barnard. 'How are you settling in?'

'Fine,' said Holly. Which was not quite true. Starting a new school in mid-term was proving a bit difficult. Everyone seemed to have found themselves their little groups and friendships already and she was feeling left out of things. 'I was wondering what sort of painting you'd like us to look at.'

'That's up to you,' said Mr Barnard. 'Like I said, there are lots of old paintings around the school. Pick one that takes your fancy. Have a good look round; it'll give you the chance to get to know the old place.' He smiled. 'You'll soon fit in.'

Holly already had her first plan for fitting in worked out, and during morning break she set off to find the library.

The Winifred Bowen-Davies School was a large greystone Victorian building full of character, near the picturesque old centre of the town – the part of Willow Dale that Holly had loved at first sight. Narrow streets full of old shops that seemed unchanged by the passing years. Little back roads of sleepy cottages and curious houses. Places that Holly was looking forward to exploring, with or without Jamie.

Not that Willow Dale was all like that. The town had spread itself out over the years, and the modern outskirts boasted new houses and a large shopping centre. And, as Holly had noticed when her mother had first driven the family up there to show them the cottage where they would be living, a multiplex cinema and an ice rink.

There was a boy standing by the notice board in the library, running his finger down a list of names. It looked like a football team.

'Great,' he said. 'I'm in.' He looked round at Holly.

'I'm looking for Stephanie Smith, the editor of the school magazine,' said Holly. 'I was told she might be in here.'

'Steffie?' He waved his arm towards the far side of the library. 'She'll be lurking around back there, I expect,' he said.

'Thanks.' Holly made her way past the tall shelves of books. Right at the back of the library she found a girl sitting at a table, blonde cropped head down as she typed into a word processor. The table was covered in scribbled-on sheets of paper.

'Excuse me,' said Holly.

'Wait, can't you,' snapped the girl. 'Can't you see I'm busy?'

'Sorry,' said Holly. The girl continued to type for a minute or so. Holly looked around. The library seemed well stocked. She wondered if they had any mystery novels. Holly's great passion was for mysteries. She had managed to fill an entire crate with her book collection when they had moved.

'Well?' asked Steffie, finally looking up at Holly with staring pale blue eyes.

'I'd like to help on the magazine,' said Holly. 'I used to edit the magazine back at my old school in Highgate – in London.'

Steffie leaned back, her sharp, icy eyes giving Holly the once-over in a very unfriendly fashion. 'You're from London, are you?' she said. 'I suppose you've come here thinking you can improve things.'

'Not at all,' said Holly, surprised by Steffie's remark. 'I just wanted to help out.'

'I don't think we need another editor,' said Steffie. 'I've been doing it for two terms now, and I've just got it the way I want it.'

Holly didn't comment on this. She had seen a recent issue of the magazine and she'd spotted a lot of things about it that she felt could be improved. Like the title, for instance. *Winformation* sounded terribly cutesy to Holly. This didn't seem an appropriate time to mention it, though.

'I don't mind what I do,' said Holly. 'Articles, reviews. Anything you say.'

'There's a hockey match on Wednesday. You could do a write-up of that, if you like.'

'Fine,' said Holly.

'I'll need it first thing Thursday morning,' said Steffie. 'And if it's no good it won't get in. OK? I have the final say over everything that goes in the magazine.'

'Fair enough,' said Holly, privately thinking the opposite. She smiled. 'It'll be good, don't worry.'

Steffie started typing into her machine again. 'That's for me to decide,' she said.

Crumbs, thought Holly, leaving the spiky girl to her typing, *I don't think I'm going to enjoy working with her very much*.

She met up with Jamie at the gates at the end of school. He was with a group of boys. They were talking animatedly about computer games.

'You coming, Jamie?' she asked, after standing unnoticed by him for a while.

'Later,' said Jamie, diving straight back into the discussion.

Holly walked home alone. Despite all his protests over the move from London, it looked as if Jamie hadn't lost any time in finding himself some new friends.

The Adams family had moved into a four-bedroom cottage where the old town and the new town met. The estate agent had described it as 'full of potential'. Meanwhile, before they could live there comfortably it needed rewiring, the plumbing needed sorting out and the whole place was crying out to be redecorated and modernised from top to bottom.

A couple of workmen were digging a long trench by the front path. Holly's father was standing at the open front door.

'We'll be trailing mud in and out for months at

this rate,' he said. 'It's a good job there are no carpets in the hall yet. Where's Jamie?'

'I left him chatting with some boys,' said Holly.

'See?' said Mr Adams. 'I told him it wouldn't take him five minutes to make new friends. And after all that bother.' He smiled at her. 'Come and look at this.'

He took her round to the shed in the garden. His workbench and lathe were already set up in there, and his carpentry tools were in neat rows, lying on new shelves or hanging from hooks on the walls.

'What do you think?' he said. 'I'll soon be in full production.' He rubbed his hands together like a small boy with a new train set. 'Exciting, isn't it?'

Holly laughed. It was nice to see her father smiling and happy. No more coming home late and exhausted from the office where he had worked as a lawyer. A very successful lawyer, but a lawyer who had always wanted to spend his time working with his hands. Carpentry had been a hobby in London, but the move to Willow Dale had given him the opportunity to concentrate on the work he loved doing.

Holly went into the house and up to her room. 'Our priorities,' her mother had said, 'are to get the bedrooms finished. Then at least we've all got somewhere to retreat to from the chaos.'

Holly had already put her posters and photographs up, making the new room hers as soon as possible. And her books were on the shelves. *All*

15

her books. Back in London her bedroom had only been half the size, and she had been forced to keep some of her books in boxes under the bed. But now she could have her entire collection on display.

Over dinner she told her parents about her encounter with Steffie Smith.

'I'll tell you what *that* sounds like to me,' her mother said. 'It sounds like someone who's not very sure of herself.'

'That's what I thought,' said Holly. 'And the magazine isn't brilliant, either. I've already seen lots of things I'd change if I was in charge.'

'I hope you didn't tell her that,' said her father.

'Of course not,' said Holly. 'I was very polite. It's a pity though. It was always fun working on the magazine with Miranda. I'm not sure this is going to be any sort of fun at all.' She sighed. 'And it's not as easy making new friends as I'd hoped.'

Miranda Hunt had been Holly's best friend back in Highgate. Together they had haunted the bookshops and library, searching out the mystery novels that they both loved to read. They had agreed to write regularly to each other, and Miranda had actually handed Holly her first letter the evening before they had left. 'It'll be something to read on the way up to Yorkshire,' Miranda had said, and Holly had laughed over the long letter. It had almost been like having Miranda in the car with her.

'Can I leave the table?' asked Jamie. 'I've been

invited round to Philip's house to play Devil Riders on his computer.'

'So long as Philip's parents don't mind,' said Mrs Adams.

'Of course they don't,' said Jamie, already half-way out of the room. 'Philip's always got friends round. See you later.'

'Don't be late,' shouted Mr Adams.

Holly sighed again. 'No one's invited me round to play on their computer,' she said.

'You don't like computer games,' said her father.

'That's not the point,' said Holly.

'Are you having trouble finding new friends?' asked her mother sympathetically. 'I know how you feel. It's not easy for me to find my feet in my new bank. Everyone seems to think I've come up from London intending to change everything.'

'You wanted to run your own branch,' said Holly's father. 'You've been working for this promotion for the last five years.'

'I know,' said her mother. 'I'm not complaining. I'm just sympathising with Holly's position.'

'Why don't you scout round and see what clubs there are at school that you could join?' suggested Mr Adams. 'That's always a good way of making friends.'

'That's a thought,' said Holly. 'Or I could even start my own club. A club for people who like mystery novels. I know Miranda and I said we'd send each other books with our letters, but it's not the same as *being* with someone.'

'There's your answer, then,' said her father. 'Set up your own club.'

Later that evening Holly was in her room. One of the first things she had done when she had arrived in Willow Dale was to go out and buy herself a new notebook. She always liked to write her thoughts and ideas down.

She opened the brand new red notebook on her desk.

I can put an advertisement in the school magazine, she thought. That was the best way of getting recruits for a new club.

She sketched out a short piece:

Do you enjoy a good mystery? Do you like reading mystery novels? Then join The Mystery Club. Lots of fun. Discussions. Book-swapping. Writing our own mysteries. Contact Holly Adams, Form 4b – Friday lunch-time.

That should do it, said Holly to herself. *I'd certainly respond to an advert like that.*

She gazed out of the window, over the long garden and the tall green trees. In the distance she could see the misty Yorkshire hills on the horizon.

She closed her notebook. *I wonder who will come?* she thought to herself. *Friendlier people than Steffie Smith, I hope.*

2 The advert

The next edition of *Winformation* appeared first
thing on Friday morning. Holly eagerly turned to
the back page to check that Steffie had included her
advertisement.

She had. Sort of.

The advert read, 'The Mystery Club. Form 4b,
Friday lunch-time.' And that was it. Sandwiched
in between someone wanting to sell some football
boots and an article about a jumble sale to help
towards the new gym.

For heaven's sake, thought Holly. *Where's the rest
of it? Who's going to bother responding to something as
vague as that?*

Despondently she turned the pages, searching
for her hockey match report. She had worked hard
on that. It had taken her most of Wednesday night
to polish it up into something that she felt sure
Steffie couldn't refuse to publish.

She found it and started reading. Holly prided
herself on her writing – even to the extent of
having dreams of becoming a journalist when
she left school. That would be a marvellous job –

spending her time investigating complicated crimes and terrible murders.

Steffie, it seemed, had been at her report with a butcher's knife. She had cut it to half its original length, and had even changed the bits she *had* left in. It hardly looked like the same report at all.

Holly went straight to the library at break, determined to give Steffie Smith a piece of her mind. But the desk was empty.

Hiding won't help you, thought Holly. *I'll find you eventually. And when I do, watch out!*

Meanwhile she still had to find a painting to write about for the homework Mr Barnard had set.

The front entrance to the school with its broad steps and its impressive double doors led into a wide hall lined with cabinets full of medals and cups and ribbons. There were a few chairs for visitors. Around the walls, and along the wood-panelled corridor which led off from the rear of the hallway, hung heavy-framed paintings.

Some were landscapes showing the beautiful Yorkshire countryside with its craggy hills, plunging valleys with tumble-watered rivers flowing in their deep laps, the huge sky full of menacing clouds looming over tiny cottages.

It was a land full of mystery to Holly, so very different from the crowded streets and the flat horizons of London, with its jutting office blocks and its endless noise and bustle. Not that Holly hadn't liked living in London. She had grown up in all the activity of a big city and was used to the pace of life there. But here in Willow Dale, it felt like being at home and on holiday all at the same time.

All she needed were a few friends and she'd be completely happy.

She stood in front of the largest of all the paintings. It was one of a series of portraits of people who had been involved with the school over the years. But this one was twice the size of all the others. It was a portrait of Winifred Bowen-Davies herself, the founder of the school, clad in a black high-necked dress brightened only by some flecks of white on the bodice. She sat enthroned upon a heavily carved dark wood chair. Her severe eyes frowned down upon Holly from a fierce, intelligent, autocratic face framed with brushed-back grey hair.

Holly felt glad that the present headteacher, Miss Horswell, seemed a much kinder, more cheerful sort of person.

But there was *something* about Winifred's face that she liked. Something dependable.

Holly came to a decision. She would write her art homework on this portrait of Winifred Bowen-Davies herself. And what would be even more interesting would be to try and find out more about Winifred's life. Portraits always meant more when you knew something about the person being depicted.

There was a leaflet about the school. It had been

given to her at her interview with Miss Horswell, but she hadn't read it yet. There didn't seem to have been the time. Perhaps she'd have a few minutes to look through it at lunch-time while she was waiting for her Mystery Club recruits to arrive.

As she sat alone in the form room at lunch-time, anxiously hoping that *someone* might arrive in response to her advert, Holly read through the leaflet.

The school, she discovered, had been founded in 1860. But there wasn't much about Winifred.

Perhaps she's got a mysterious past, thought Holly. Now *that* would be worth finding out about!

Holly looked up at the clock. Time was ticking steadily away. Ten minutes ago a boy's face had appeared around the door. Holly had jumped up, but before she had time to say anything the face had disappeared.

Every time she heard footsteps in the corridor she looked up hopefully. Surely someone would be interested?

Holly began to have severe doubts about her Mystery Club plans. She took out Miranda's letter and read through it again to cheer herself up.

Holly sighed, folding the letter into her pocket and wondering whether it was worth sitting alone in the empty form room much longer.

Five more minutes, she thought. *Then I'll give up*.

It was beginning to look as though the Mystery

Club was going to have a grand membership total of one.

'Hi! Is this the right place for the Mystery Club?'

Holly looked up. A smiling girl was standing in the doorway. She had short blonde hair and a happy, attractive face. A sports bag was slung over her shoulder, the handle of a tennis racket poking out of the top.

'I'm hoping it *will* be,' said Holly. 'If anyone turns up.'

'Great,' said the girl, bounding into the room. 'I'm Tracy Foster. You're new, aren't you?' There was a lilt to her voice, a slight accent that Holly couldn't quite place.

'That's right. I'm Holly Adams.'

'Hi, Holly.' Tracy flung her bag on to a chair and perched on top of a desk. 'So? What's the deal? Who's running this club?'

'Me, I hope,' said Holly.

'Oh, right. You put the ad in the magazine, did you?' Tracy gave her a big grin. 'It was kind of intriguing. The Mystery Club. Great name. So what sort of mysteries does it involve?'

'I thought it would be good to get some people together who like mystery novels, or mysteries in general,' said Holly. 'Do you read much?'

'All the time,' said Tracy brightly. 'But I'm into other things as well. I'm in nearly every club in the school. I should be at tennis right now,

23

but it got cancelled. So you like mystery novels, do you?'

Holly nodded, liking the girl immediately. 'They're my absolute favourites.' She had placed the accent. 'Are you American?' she asked.

'Half,' said Tracy. 'My dad is American, but Mom is English. Is my accent that bad? I thought I'd got rid of most of it. I've been over here for three years now.' She gave a small shrug, glancing out of the window. 'Ever since my folks got divorced.' She smiled again. 'Mom runs a nursery here. I guess I miss California, and I really miss my dad, but you've got to go with the flow, Holly, know what I mean? Make the best of things.'

Holly nodded. 'I've only just moved here from London,' she said. 'I thought the Mystery Club would be a good way of making friends.'

'It is!' said Tracy, spreading her arms. 'You've met *me*.'

Holly gave another laugh. 'You're interested in joining then?'

'Where do I sign?' said Tracy.

Holly laughed. 'Perhaps we should call ourselves the Mystery Duo,' she said.

Tracy swung her hand through the air. 'I can see the sign,' she said. '"Tracy Foster and Holly Adams. Mysteries are *Us*!"' She beamed at Holly. 'What do you say?'

'The biggest mystery I can think of,' said a voice

from the door, 'is why that ice cream parlour down the road is always out of chocolate chip.'

They both looked round. The girl standing there had a round face and dark brown hair that looked as if it had recently been caught in a whirlwind. She blinked at them through wire-framed spectacles and came ambling into the classroom.

'I need to join a club,' said the girl, slumping into a chair. 'My mother says I spend too much time on my own. She's told me that I should join in more.' She looked up at the two girls. 'So here I am. What's going on?'

'You're Belinda Hayes, aren't you?' said Tracy.

'That's right,' said the girl. 'And you're Tracy Foster. I keep seeing your name attached to lists of athletic events.' She looked suspiciously at Holly. 'This isn't a new sports club, is it?' she said. 'Have I made a terrible mistake?'

'It's not a sports club,' said Holly. She introduced herself.

'Thank heavens,' said Belinda. 'I don't mind humouring my mother a bit, but not to the extent of leaping around with a tennis racket or anything. I get enough exercise looking after Meltdown.' She grinned. 'Meltdown is my horse,' she explained. 'Great name, isn't it?'

'You've got your own horse?' said Holly.

Belinda nodded. 'That's where all my energy goes. Up first thing every morning. I'm sure my mother believes that horse cleans himself out, the

25

way she goes on about how lazy I am. Just because she spends her entire life dashing round, she thinks everyone should.'

She blinked from one girl to the other. 'So?' she said. 'Tell me. What exactly *is* a mystery club?'

'Not *a* mystery club,' said Tracy. '*The* Mystery Club. You'll find out if you join.'

'I thought we could talk about mystery novels,' said Holly. 'Swap books. Things like that. I've got quite a few mystery novels at home you could borrow.'

'So the idea is to sit around chatting and reading books, is it?' said Belinda.

'More or less,' said Holly.

Belinda's face broke into a broad smile. 'I think I can handle that,' she said. She heaved herself up. 'All this joining clubs stuff is making me hungry. Anyone fancy a stroll down to the ice cream parlour? There's still half an hour before afternoon classes.'

'Do they do banana flavour?' asked Holly.

'They certainly do,' said Belinda. 'And pistachio, and pineapple, and hazelnut, and walnut flake, and raspberry ripple. And the most massive chocolate nut sundaes you've ever seen.'

'With fresh cream on top,' said Tracy.

Holly's eyes lit up. 'Lead me to it,' she said. 'I didn't know what I was missing.'

'Don't you want to wait around for a bit?' said

Tracy. 'You might get some more people interested in the club.'

'We *are* the club,' said Belinda. 'Who else could we possibly need? Didn't you know? All the best things come in threes.'

Tracy grabbed up her bag and followed them. 'And we can draw up a list of ideas for the club while we're there,' she said. 'And the last one to the ice cream parlour pays the bill!'

As the three girls ran out into the open, Holly felt sure that they were going to be good friends.

Her advert in the school magazine had worked perfectly.

3   The archives

'I can't believe the number of books you've got,' said Belinda. 'How do you get time to read them all?'

'I read a lot,' admitted Holly. 'I suppose I must be a mystery addict.'

Belinda nodded. 'I'll say.' She grinned. 'I usually wait for them to come on TV.'

The three girls were in Holly's bedroom. It was Saturday afternoon. The first official meeting of the Mystery Club.

'Anyone got any thoughts about what we're actually going to do?' asked Belinda.

'I've had an idea,' said Tracy. 'Couldn't we devise our own mystery board game?'

'That would be terrific,' said Holly. 'That's just the sort of thing!'

'I could run something off on my dad's computer,' said Belinda. 'We could have clue cards and suspect cards and squares on the board where you're trapped in an old mine shaft and have to throw a six to escape.'

'And a square just before the end that sends

you all the way back to the beginning,' said Holly.

Holly opened her notebook and the three girls spent the afternoon yelling with excitement and laughter as they thought up fiendishly difficult clues and perilous adventures.

Later that afternoon Holly's mother brought them up some sandwiches and orange juice. 'I thought you'd be getting hungry,' she said. 'You sound like you've been using a lot of energy up here.'

'Thanks,' said Belinda. 'I was starving. My brain needs constant refuelling.' She picked up a sandwich. 'It's not easy being as clever as I am all the time.'

'Did you remember to ask Tracy and Belinda about Winifred Bowen-Davies?' Mrs Adams reminded Holly.

'Oh, no,' said Holly. 'It slipped my mind completely.'

Mrs Adams left them to it.

'What did you want to know?' asked Tracy.

Holly told her about the homework Mr Barnard had set. 'There doesn't seem to be anything about Winifred in any of the school papers,' said Holly. 'Do either of you know anything about her?'

'I know she died,' Belinda offered helpfully.

'Really?' said Tracy drily. 'I didn't even know she'd been ill.'

'I'd like to find out more about her,' said Holly.

'Especially if she's got a mysterious past. I could
write a piece for the school magazine about her.'

'You'd have to get it past Steffie,' said Tracy. 'She
never seems too keen on letting other people write
things. You'd think she owned the magazine the
way she behaves.'

'I'll write something brilliant,' said Holly. 'But I
need to think of some way of finding out about
Winifred Bowen-Davies.'

'Ask Miss Horswell,' said Tracy. 'If anyone
knows, the headteacher should.'

Holly felt she had made a good impression on Miss
Horswell during her interview, especially when she
had mentioned her hopes of becoming a journalist.
'I like a girl with ambitions,' Miss Horswell had
said. 'You come to see me if you need any help.
My door's always open.'

Mrs Williams, the school secretary, worked
in an ante-room that led to the headteacher's
office. At break on Monday morning Holly sat in
Mrs William's office, waiting until the headteacher
was free to see her.

'Holly,' said Miss Horswell with a smile. 'Come
on in. What can I do for you? No problems, I
hope?'

'No,' said Holly. 'Nothing like that. I'm doing an
essay on the painting of Winifred Bowen-Davies
that's hanging in the hall, and I wondered if
you might be able to tell me anything about

her. There doesn't seem to be much information available.'

'That's an excellent idea,' said Miss Horswell. 'But I'm not sure that I should just *tell* you everything. I think a far better idea would be for you to do a bit of research on your own.'

'I've looked in the library,' said Holly, 'but I couldn't find anything.'

'All the old documents relating to the school are kept in a room in the basement. Documents that go right back to the last century. Ask Mrs Williams for the key. There's bound to be something interesting, although I don't think anyone's been down there for years. I certainly haven't.'

Holly found Tracy and Belinda and showed them the large bunch of keys. They both liked the idea of a lunch-time hunt through the archives.

'I'll even miss my dance class,' said Tracy. 'How's that for dedication?'

'Me too,' said Belinda.

'You don't do dance,' said Tracy. 'At least, I've never seen you there.'

Belinda shrugged. 'But if I did, I'd miss it,' she said. 'But I'll need my lunch first.'

The room certainly looked as if no one had been in it for a long time.

As Holly opened the door she could smell the musty, dusty scent of old paper. The room was half filled with free-standing shelves full of old

31

black leather-bound volumes. The rest of the room was piled with boxes overflowing with papers and folders and ancient textbooks.

'Gosh!' said Tracy. 'It's dusty down here. We'll get filthy.'

'All in a good cause,' said Holly. 'This is our first real mystery. The grim secret of Winifred Bowen-Davies.'

'Look at this,' said Belinda, reaching up to wipe the dust off a thick old book. 'Look at the date: 1912. Even my mother wasn't alive then.'

'This one's even older,' said Tracy. '1891.' She heaved at it, nearly collapsing under the weight as she hauled it off the shelf.

The old books proved fascinating reading. Taking a book each the three girls spent half an hour carefully wading through the dry old pages with their browned and wrinkled edges.

Holly closed the book she had been reading. 'These aren't really helping us with Winifred, are they?' she said. She walked over to the piles of boxes. 'I'm beginning to wonder if we're going to find anything useful at all.'

'Me too,' said Belinda, wiping a stray lock of hair off her forehead with a grimy hand. 'There's just too much of it.'

Tracy started nosing through the boxes. She found some old black and white photographs of ranks of schoolgirls in ancient, heavy-looking uniforms lined up in the playground. 'Look at the hats they had to wear!' she said. 'And look at the teachers. They've all got gowns on. Can you imagine our teachers all having to go around in gowns? They'd look like a bunch of mad bats.'

'There are some framed pictures over here,' said Holly. They were stacked behind the boxes. She leaned over to try and pull some out, but they were too tightly wedged. 'Lend a hand,' she said.

The three girls worked to drag the boxes out of the way. Some of the older ones fell to pieces, scattering their contents on the floor.

'No one's touched any of this stuff for years,' said Belinda, crouching to gather the spilled papers together.

Holly edged herself into the gap and pulled up a framed print. A row of teachers stared grimly at her through the dusty, brown-pocked glass.

'What's that?' said Tracy, pointing towards the floor at Holly's feet.

It was a roll of something tied up with string. Holly picked it up. It was about a metre long and quite heavy.

'It's canvas,' she said.

'Let's open it up,' said Tracy. 'It might be something interesting.'

They laid the thick roll on the floor. 'We'll need something to cut the string,' said Tracy. 'We'll never get all those knots undone.'

'I'll do it,' said Belinda. 'I'm good with difficult knots.' She crouched and picked at the tangled string with her fingernails. The other two stood watching as the strands of string gradually came loose. Very carefully Belinda unrolled the canvas.

'Wow!' she said. 'It's a painting.'

They weighted the corners of the canvas with books and stood back to have a proper look.

It was a portrait of a woman. She was wearing a very old-fashioned white dress covered with delicate frills. She was standing in what looked like the garden of a manor house. The house itself was away in the background. On the left of the painting was a smaller house, and on the right an odd-looking circular building that seemed to be just a ring of stone pillars with a tall, flat roof on top.

The woman was staring solemnly out of the painting, her skin so pale it was almost white, her long ash-blonde hair heaped and piled on her head. She had the palest, saddest eyes Holly had ever seen.

'I wonder who she is,' said Holly.

'She looks like she's having a pretty miserable time of it, whoever she is,' said Belinda.

'Whoever she *was*,' said Tracy. 'Look at her clothes. This must have been painted years ago. I mean, years and *years* ago!'

Holly's eyes widened. 'I wonder if anyone knows this is down here?' she said. 'Miss Horswell said no one's been down here for an age. I've seen programmes on television where people have found old paintings in their attics, and when they've taken them to experts they've discovered that they're worth a fortune. You don't think . . .'

'Don't get carried away,' said Belinda. 'You don't seriously think this would have been stuffed down here if it was worth anything, do you?'

'But you never know,' said Tracy. 'I mean, things like that *do* happen. And it's obviously very old. Is it signed?'

They searched for a signature. 'Here we are,' said Holly, moving the book that held down the left hand corner of the painting. 'Oh. That's not much help.' Spidery black letters read 'R.B. after H.B.'

'What do you think that means?' said Holly.

'I vote we take it up to Miss Horswell,' said Tracy. 'Even if it isn't valuable, it's a shame to leave it down here. It ought to be on show somewhere.'

'And if it is worth a lot of money,' said Holly, 'would get our pictures in the newspapers. "Student sleuths discover lost masterpiece." We'd be famous.'

'It's not going to be worth a fortune,' said Belinda. 'I'll bet you any money you like. Still, like Tracy says, we might as well rescue it now we've found it.'

Carefully locking the door, the three girls made their way up to ground level.

'Look at the state of us!' said Tracy. 'We're filthy!'

They took a detour to the cloakroom. They did their best to get the grime off, but dust and dirt were still clinging to their clothes as they headed for Miss Horswell's office.

Mr Barnard was in the outer office, talking to Mrs Williams.

'Look what we've found,' said Holly excitedly. 'You'll know what it's worth, won't you, sir?'

'Well, well,' said Mr Barnard. 'You look like you've been down a coal mine.'

'We've been in the basement,' said Holly. 'We found this.'

They unrolled the painting on the desk. The sad-eyed woman gazed up at them.

'Very nice,' said Mr Barnard, leaning closely over it.

'But is it valuable?' asked Holly.

'I shouldn't think so,' said Mr Barnard. 'See this?' He pointed to the signature. 'When someone writes "after", it means it's a copy of an original. Probably a pupil here did this a few years ago.'

'Oh!' said Holly disappointedly. 'So it won't be worth much?'

'I'm afraid not.' Mr Barnard smiled. 'Nice try, though.'

Miss Horswell's door opened. 'There's a lot of activity out here,' she said. She spotted the painting. 'Good heavens!' she said. '*The White Lady*. Well I never.' She stared at the painting. 'I'd quite forgotten about it.'

'It's a copy of an original,' said Mr Barnard. 'I

36

think the girls here hoped it might be worth a bit of money.'

Miss Horswell nodded. 'They might be right,' she said. 'If the mystery of the White Lady could be solved, it would be worth a great deal of money indeed.'

Holly grinned at Belinda. 'See?' she said. 'What did I tell you.' She looked at Miss Horswell. 'Will you tell us about the mystery?' she asked. 'I'm dying to know.'

The three girls looked at the painting and then at Miss Horswell, waiting for her to explain what she had meant.

Just then the bell sounded for afternoon lessons.

'You'd better be off about your business,' said Miss Horswell. 'You don't want to be late for your lessons.' She looked at the disappointed faces of the three girls. 'I'll tell you what,' she said. 'You come back here at the end of school and if I've got time I'll tell you about it then. Now then, off you go. And I'd recommend a visit to the washrooms, girls. Your parents will think I've had you labouring in the fields all day if you go home with your clothes in that state.'

4   The White Lady

It was difficult for Holly to concentrate on her schoolwork that afternoon. Especially as she was sitting next to Tracy for one lesson, and Tracy was constantly slipping her pieces of paper with solutions to the mystery scribbled on them.

'The White Lady was a pupil at the school years ago,' suggested one of Tracy's pieces of paper. 'She failed all her exams and was bricked up in a basement room as a punishment.'

Holly scribbled back, 'No. She was a teacher who had a tragic love affair with a prince and threw herself off the top of the school. She was buried in a secret grave somewhere in the school grounds with all the prince's love letters. If they're found it will cause a major scandal!'

The three girls arrived together in Mrs Williams's office. Mr Barnard was already there.

'I'm as interested in the mystery as you are,' he said. 'You don't mind me joining in, I hope?'

'Of course not,' said Holly. 'But *we're* going to solve it.'

'I very much doubt that,' said Miss Horswell,

looking out of her office door. 'Come along in, all of you. I can spare you ten minutes.'

She had the painting laid out on a table, weighted down by a few ornaments.

They crowded around the table. 'Now then,' said Miss Horswell. 'As Mr Barnard has already told you, this is only a copy of the original. Shortly after this school was founded, the original *White Lady* was donated to us by a gentleman called Hugo Bastable, the owner of Woodfree Abbey. He was a famous artist at the time. The initials here,' she pointed to the bottom of the painting. '"H.B." That stands for Hugo Bastable, you see.'

'I know Woodfree Abbey,' said Belinda. 'It's a big old place not far from here. It's open to the public. I've been there.'

'That's right,' said Miss Horswell. 'Although it's no longer owned by the Bastables. The story goes that one Roderick Bastable, Hugo's grandson, let the Abbey go to rack and ruin. He preferred to spend his time frittering away the family fortune on wild enterprises and on running up huge gambling debts. He tried to save himself by demanding that the school return his grandfather's painting. But Hugo Bastable had insisted that the painting should be kept by the school as a nest egg, only to be sold if the school found itself in dire financial straits.' Miss Horswell smiled. 'As you can imagine, Roderick was not at all pleased by this. Shortly after this, there was

39

a burglary at the school and the painting was stolen.'

'Stolen by Roderick!' said Holly.

'Very probably,' said Miss Horswell. 'But his plans for making any money out of the painting, if he *did* steal it, were thrown into disarray when he was arrested and convicted for fraud. It was while he was in prison that he painted a copy of the *White Lady*. From memory. The Bastables were a very artistic family, although Roderick preferred to spend his time in other ways. You see, Roderick had found out that he was dying. He knew he would never get out of prison. He made a copy of the *White Lady*.' Miss Horswell gestured to the painting. 'This very copy, in fact.' All eyes turned to the painting.

'The legend goes,' Miss Horswell continued, 'that he added various clues to guide his daughter to the missing painting. That way, even if he never got the benefit of it, his family would be able to unearth the *White Lady* and get out of the financial troubles he had left them in. Unfortunately for Roderick, the Bastables lost control of the Abbey, and all chance of them finding the painting was gone.'

'So the original of the *White Lady* was never found?' breathed Holly.

'Never,' said Miss Horswell. 'After Roderick died the copy hung for a while in the Abbey. But the new owners soon wanted rid of it. News had leaked out about the mystery. People came from all over to try and solve the clues and find the missing painting. They caused quite a nuisance, as you can imagine. In the end, the people who owned the Abbey gave this copy to us, hoping that it would put a stop to all the treasure hunters it had been attracting. Although the original was very valuable, Roderick's copy was virtually worthless. The headteacher at the time hung the copy in this office. But I had them take it down when I first took over. She has such a sad face, I think. I couldn't bear to have her looking down at me all the time while I worked.'

'And the mystery was never solved?' said Holly.

'Never,' said Miss Horswell. She smiled. 'There you are,' she said. 'Now you know all there is to know about the *White Lady*.'

Tracy leaned over the painting. 'Do you know where the clues are?' she said. 'Is it like one of those pictures with things hidden in it?'

'I have no idea,' said Miss Horswell.

'Could we keep it for a while?' asked Holly. 'I'd love to try and find the clues.'

'You're welcome to try,' said Miss Horswell. 'So long as I don't have to look at that poor woman's face every day when I come to work, I don't mind what you do.'

'We can keep it in the art room,' said Mr Barnard. 'You can come and study it whenever you get a free moment. How's that?'

The three girls left Miss Horswell's office, filled with excitement.

Mrs Williams was standing in the hall with her coat on.

'There was a man asking to see you, Mr Barnard,' she said. 'I told him you were busy, but he was very insistent. I think he's waiting outside.'

'Did he say who he was?' asked Mr Barnard.

'He wouldn't leave a name.'

A frown flickered across Mr Barnard's face for a second. 'You girls go on up to the art room,' he said. 'I won't be a minute.'

He headed for the entrance and walked quickly down the steps. Holly and her friends walked upstairs.

'You don't seriously believe that after all these years we're going to be able to discover something that no one else has noticed, do you?' said Belinda as they entered the art room.

'If you're so sure it's a waste of time, you can always go home,' said Tracy.

'What? And leave it to you? We're guaranteed to get nowhere if I do that,' said Belinda. 'Someone with brains should be involved.'

They spread the painting out on one of the tables in the art room.

'Perhaps if we could find out what those houses in the background are it might be a start,' said Holly.

'That's easy,' said Belinda. 'It's Woodfree Abbey.

I've been there a couple of times with my parents. The house and grounds are open to the public. They do these wonderful scones in the cafeteria in there. Full of cream and jam. It's worth going there just for them.' She looked at the painting. 'I can't see any clues here at all.'

'Of course you can't,' said Holly. 'If they were obvious the mystery would have been solved years ago.'

'So,' said Tracy. 'If that big building in the background is the Abbey – what are these other two?'

'I think that's the summer-house,' said Belinda, pointing to the house on the left of the White Lady. 'But I'm not sure about the other thing. It looks like a wedding cake. I haven't been to the Abbey since I was about ten,' she admitted. 'I don't remember much about it, really – other than the scones!'

'Perhaps we should go there,' said Holly.

'I wonder what those are,' said Belinda, pointing to a pattern of upright lines, crosses and diagonal lines that marched along the wall just beneath the roof of the summer-house.

'Just decorations,' said Tracy. 'Hey! Perhaps he buried the painting right under where she's standing.'

'Well, they're not going to let us dig the place up,' said Holly. 'You heard what Miss Horswell said. The owners are fed up with treasure hunters all over the place.'

'But that was years ago,' said Tracy. 'I shouldn't think anyone's had a good look round for ages.'

'That's a gorgeous brooch she's wearing,' said Holly. It was a black and white bird with a long tail. 'Maybe that's a clue?'

'Everything might be a clue,' said Belinda. 'I think you're right – we should go there and have a good look around. Maybe eat a scone or two . . .'

'Perhaps we should take a photo of the painting?' suggested Tracy. 'If we each had a copy of a photo, we wouldn't have to keep coming back here to look at it. I know someone who could help us. You two wait here, I'll see if I can find him.' Tracy ran out of the art room.

'She does dash around, doesn't she?' said Belinda. 'I don't know where she gets the energy from.' She sat down. 'And she's probably the sort who keeps her bedroom spotlessly tidy as well.' She grinned. 'Unlike me.'

After a few minutes Tracy came back into the art room with a tall, blonde-haired boy.

'This is Kurt Welford,' she said. 'He's agreed to take the photo for us. He's really good at photography, aren't you, Kurt? When he's not playing cricket.' She smiled. 'He's cricket mad.'

Kurt laughed. 'I don't know about cricket *mad*,' he said. 'But photography definitely comes second.'

'Kurt's dad is the editor of the *Willow Dale Express*,' said Tracy. 'Kurt has had photographs published in it,' said Tracy. 'He's even got his own darkroom at home.' Tracy led Kurt over to the painting. 'This is what I was telling you about,' she said. 'Could you take a picture of it and let us have a copy print each?'

'I don't see why not,' said Kurt. 'Someone will have to hold it up for me, and you'll probably get a bit of a flare from the flash, but it ought to come out reasonably well.'

He took the camera out of its case. Tracy and Holly held the painting between them.

'I'll take a couple,' said Kurt. 'Just to be on the safe side.'

The camera flashed twice.

'How soon can we have them?' asked Tracy.

'This is the end of a roll,' said Kurt. 'I could print them out this afternoon and bring them in tomorrow morning.'

'That would be great,' said Tracy.

'What do you want the photos for?' asked Kurt.

'That's a secret,' said Holly. 'We're going to solve a mystery. You'll find out soon enough once we've worked it all out – and then you can take a photo of us for the *Express*.'

Kurt laughed. 'I've got to go,' he said. 'I'll see you in the morning with the prints.'

'Is he your boyfriend?' asked Belinda after he had left.

'We go out together sometimes,' said Tracy. 'It's nothing deadly serious.'

As they were speaking Mr Barnard came into the room. 'Sorry, girls,' he said. 'I'm going to have to lock up now. Something has come up. You can look at the painting again tomorrow.'

They walked out of the school gates. While they were standing chatting on the corner before going their separate ways home, Holly saw Mr Barnard come out of the school and cross towards a grey car that was parked on the far side of the road.

A man was standing by the car with his back to them. As Holly watched, the man climbed into the driving seat. He was quite a distance away, and she couldn't be absolutely certain, but Holly thought she saw an eagle printed on the back of his leather jacket.

Mr Barnard opened the passenger door and Holly saw him glance anxiously around, as if he were nervous of being seen getting into the car.

'Right,' said Belinda. 'I'll find out the opening times of the Abbey from my mother, and the first chance we get, we'll go over there. Is that a deal?'

'And tomorrow,' said Tracy, 'we can start looking properly at the *White Lady*, and figure out some of the clues.'

Holly nodded absent-mindedly. She was still thinking about the anxious look she had seen on Mr Barnard's face. Perhaps the strange man had brought some bad news?

The car drove away from them.

'Holly?' said Tracy. 'Are you paying attention?'

46

'Sorry,' said Holly. 'I was just wondering what made Mr Barnard rush off like that. I hope it's nothing serious. I like Mr Barnard.'

'Can we concentrate on what we're supposed to be talking about?' said Tracy. 'About the painting?'

'Yes, sorry,' said Holly. 'First thing tomorrow we'll start searching for those clues.' She smiled. 'I quite fancy the idea of getting my picture in the *Express*,' she said. 'Perhaps I could even write an article about it.'

'You're getting ahead of yourself a bit, aren't you?' said Belinda. 'We haven't even started looking yet, and you've got an article planned.'

'I like to think ahead,' said Holly.

On her way home she was already imagining her article for the local newspaper: *New girl in Willow Dale solves age-old mystery*.

Now that would be something to write to Miranda about.

5 Woodfree Abbey

'Why did you ask me to write a report of that hockey match if you were going to change it so much?' Holly demanded. She had finally caught up with Steffie Smith.

Steffie was in the corridor, looking very busy with a stack of folders in her arms. She didn't look as if she wanted to stop. 'It's your own fault,' she said. 'You shouldn't have made it so long. It wouldn't have fitted in.'

'You could have told me how many words you wanted,' said Holly.

Steffie smiled coldly at her. 'You should have asked.'

'Now, wait a minute . . .'

Steffie shrugged. 'I haven't got time to argue about this. The editor's decision is final. You know *that*, surely?' She turned and walked off.

Holly followed her.

'We haven't made a very good start, have we?' Holly said as calmly as she could. 'Look, I only want to help. Perhaps I could write something else? I'll keep it short. I found a painting in the basement.

There's a very interesting story behind it. Shall I do a piece on that?'

'A painting?' said Steffie, laughing. 'I'm sure everyone will be thrilled to read about a *painting*.' She frowned at Holly, obviously wanting to get rid of her. 'OK,' she said. 'Write something about that. By Thursday.'

Kurt had been as good as his word with the prints of the photographs he had taken. He had given them to Tracy, who had handed one each to Belinda and Holly. They weren't perfect, but they were certainly good enough to show most of the details, and it would save them having to refer constantly to the original, especially during their planned trip to Woodfree Abbey.

They had decided on their visit to the Abbey. Belinda had found out that the house and grounds were open until five thirty on weekdays, which gave them plenty of time to go and have a look round after school.

That afternoon the three of them caught the bus out of Willow Dale. It was a lovely sunny day. A few shreds of white cloud scudded across the blue sky and the treetops were rippling in the breeze. It was the sort of day that made Holly glad to be out in the countryside.

They got off the bus and Holly took a deep breath of the fresh air. The signs pointed down a long, steeply sloping gravel roadway between high banks of trees.

'It's kind of odd that they should call this place "Woodfree" when there are so many trees about,' said Tracy.

'Apparently in Old English, the word "wood" actually meant "mad"', said Belinda. 'So it really means "mad-free" Abbey.'

The other two looked at her.

She shrugged. 'I read it in the guide,' she said. 'I suppose the people who built the place meant that it would be free from the mad rat race. Something like that. Far from the madding crowd.'

The path took them into a deep valley. Running along the bottom of the dip was a high brick wall, punctuated by tall black iron gates. The gates were open and beyond them was a wide, flat space for cars to park. A green tree-studded hillside rose steeply in front of them.

'It's right up there,' said Belinda gloomily. 'I remember the climb. It's murder.'

'Nonsense,' said Tracy. 'The exercise will do you good. Holly, you remembered to bring the notebook, didn't you?'

'Of course I did,' said Holly. They had jotted down all their thoughts about the possible clues in the *White Lady* in their red notebook. They hoped that something would leap out at them while they were looking around.

Tracy ran at the hillside. 'Last one up is a feeble old sloth!' she shouted.

'A feeble *young* sloth, if you don't mind,' shouted

Belinda. She looked at Holly. 'I hope she's not going to be like this all the time,' she said. 'I get tired just watching her.'

Holly laughed, running after her lively friend. She couldn't catch Tracy, but the two of them left Belinda toiling up the slope as they ran for the lofty horizon.

'What on earth . . .?' As Holly climbed she saw something very strange coming into sight beyond the hilltop. Something smooth and curved and bright red. At first she thought it was the domed roof of a building, except that it was moving slightly from side to side. A large tent, she thought.

Tracy stood on the hilltop. 'Wow!' she exclaimed, her American accent increasing with her excitement. 'Look at this!'

Breathlessly, Holly stood at her side. The red dome had revealed itself as a huge hot air balloon. They could hear the roar as the gas jets pumped heated air up into the swelling, billowing balloon. A small crowd of people were gathered around it. The balloon was anchored to the ground with sturdy ropes and there were two men in the basket that sat on the grass beneath it.

'Wouldn't you just love to go up in one of those?' said Tracy. 'Let's have a closer look. Perhaps they're giving rides.'

She ran down the shallow green slope.

Holly waited for Belinda, who finally arrived at

the top, red-faced and out of breath. 'Now what?' she said. 'Doesn't that girl ever slow down?'

They followed Tracy down towards the balloon. It was almost full now, and the gas jets were being turned on and off as the basket rocked and skidded on the grass.

Tracy had pushed her way right to the front of the crowd and they could see her talking to one of the men in the basket. He was leaning over the side to speak to her.

She made her way back to the other two. 'They're not going up,' she said disappointedly. 'The wind's too strong. They're just testing it.'

They stood watching the balloon as it strained against its ropes, seemingly eager to pull itself free and sail away up into the blue.

'Shouldn't we be having a scout round?' said Belinda. 'That's what we came for.'

'I guess so,' said Tracy, reluctantly taking her eyes off the balloon. 'OK, Belinda, you've been here before. Where do we go?'

Belinda pointed. The house itself lay only a few hundred yards away, its white stone façade shining in the sunlight, scores of windows sparkling and gleaming. Steps led up to a huge entrance, lined with stone pillars topped with a triangular pediment.

'We need to go round to the back,' she told them.

Long smooth gardens stretched out behind the house.

'That's the summer-house,' said Belinda. 'You know? Like in the painting? And *that*' – she pointed to a circle of tall pillars, like a wedding cake – 'is the thingy.'

The summer-house, a long low building nestled in amongst trees, looked a lot more dilapidated than in the painting. Its windows were boarded up and paint was peeling from the woodwork. The roof sagged and was pocked with moss. It didn't look as if it had been used for a long time.

They walked down the gardens and turned.

'This is about it,' said Holly, taking out her photograph and holding it up for them all to see. 'This would be just about where the White Lady would have been standing.' She took their red notebook out. 'OK,' she said. 'What ideas have we got?'

The other two girls looked over her shoulders. They had all added to the notes about the painting.

'That summer-house was in better nick in those days,' said Belinda. 'And, look, that's funny. See that pattern of lines and crosses that's running along the top of the wall just under the roof? It's in the photo, but not on the actual summer-house.'

'It might just be paint lines,' said Tracy. 'It's difficult to tell what it is in the photo.'

'We'll have to have another look at the painting,' said Holly. 'But let's jot that down.' She took out a pen. 'Right,' she said. ''Pattern missing from wall

53

of summer-house." And where's this design on the roof of that building with all the pillars?' she said. 'That's not there either.'

Despite the inadequacies of Kurt's photograph, they could see that the geometric design painted on the tall roof of the strange building wasn't on the real structure. Its roof was perfectly plain white plaster.

'Write that down,' said Tracy. 'Both lots of patterns are missing.' She looked at her two friends. 'Do you think we've found some clues already?'

Belinda rolled her eyes. 'Be serious,' she said. 'If we noticed it other people must have done. It's not going to be that easy.'

'You're a real wet blanket, Belinda,' said Tracy.

'It's called being realistic,' said Belinda. 'Hello, hello. Who's this?'

A young man was walking towards them across the lawn.

'It's one of the guys from the balloon,' said Tracy.

The young man looked to be in his late teens. A lock of light brown hair hung over his forehead. He was smiling at them.

'Hello again,' he said. 'I thought I'd let you know that we're hoping to get the Red Devil up at the weekend.' He focused his bright blue eyes on Tracy. 'You said you'd like a ride? We call the balloon the Red Devil.'

Tracy's eyes widened. 'Could I?' she said. 'Honestly?'

The young man flicked his hair out of his eyes. 'Robert is in charge, but I'm sure he'd be willing to give you a ride if you're interested,' he said. 'I'm David Taylor.' He made a sweeping gesture towards the house. 'I live here. The Red Devil belongs to Robert, but we keep it here as a tourist attraction. We have coach parties on special days when we take the Red Devil up,' he said. 'We do take people up with us sometimes, and as you seemed so interested . . .'

'I am!' said Tracy.

'There would be room for all of you,' said David. He saw the dubious expression on Belinda's face. 'It's perfectly safe. We haven't lost anyone yet.'

'There's always a first time,' murmured Belinda.

'You actually live here?' said Tracy. 'I thought it was . . . well, you know, like a museum. I didn't think people lived here.'

'We keep a few rooms private,' said David. 'It's just me and my father. Although he spends most of his time working in Sheffield, so I'm on my own at the moment. Have you had a look round the old place yet?'

'Actually,' said Tracy, 'we're here to do some investigating.'

'Really?' said David. 'Do tell.'

Tracy told him all about finding the *White Lady*. Holly handed him the photograph.

David laughed. 'That old thing again?' he said. 'I thought everyone had given up on that fifty years ago. You know, there were people crawling all over this place at one time. Digging up the flower beds and poking about in all the rooms. We even had people breaking in here at night in my grandfather's time.'

'Oh,' said Tracy. 'We weren't planning on doing anything like that.'

'Have you found the clues yet?' asked David. 'There were apparently three of them.'

'The patterns on those two buildings,' said Belinda. 'The summer-house and the . . . thingy.'

'The folly,' said David. 'It's called a folly. They were very popular in the last century. You can find them in the grounds of lots of old mansions.'

'What is it?' asked Holly.

'Who knows?' said David with a smile. 'That's why such things are called follies – because no one knows what they're supposed to be. Still, it's very clever of you to have noticed about the patterns already.'

'You mean everyone already knows about them?' said Holly.

'I'm afraid so,' said David. 'I've never seen the copy of the painting myself, but if I remember correctly, those lines on the painting of the summer-house were supposed to be Roman numerals. A series of numbers. No one was able to figure out what they signified, though. And the pattern on the folly . . . well, no one really made much of that, except that people thought it might be a plan

56

of something. Like a map. But no one could work out what it might be a map of.'

'You said three clues,' said Holly.

'The third clue was something to do with the Lady herself, but I don't remember ever being told what.' He looked closely at the photograph. 'Not very cheerful, is she?' he said.

'Who was she?' asked Belinda.

'No one knows. Perhaps that's the final secret. Find out who the White Lady was, and you'll find the lost painting. I wouldn't mind finding it myself. I could do with a bit of extra money right now. Shall I see you on Saturday, then? Up, up and away in my beautiful balloon?'

'We'd love to,' said Tracy.

They watched as David walked back towards the house.

'What a smoothie,' said Belinda. 'I wouldn't trust him to fly a kite, never mind a balloon. And what was all this "we" stuff? You wouldn't get me up in one of those things if you paid me.'

As they made their way back up the gravel path to the road where they would pick up the bus back to Willow Dale, they heard the sound of a car engine and the blast of a horn.

They stepped off the path as a rusty-looking old convertible bounced past.

David Taylor was at the wheel. He gave another honk on the horn and waved. 'See you Saturday,' he shouted as the car struggled up the slope and bobbed over the top. There was the tortured grinding of gears and he was gone.

'I can understand why he'd like some more money,' said Belinda. 'That car looks as if it needs a fortune spent on it just to keep it on the road.'

'I like him,' said Tracy. 'And I'm certainly coming back for a go in the balloon, whatever you think.'

'You do that,' said Belinda. 'Meanwhile, Holly and I are going to find that missing painting, aren't we, Holly?'

'I thought you said we were wasting our time?' said Holly.

'We probably are,' said Belinda. 'But if Mr Taylor there thinks we can't do it, I'm certainly going to do my best to prove him wrong. And the first thing to do is to find out what those Roman numerals he mentioned are all about.'

6 Harry Owen

Holly sat in the art room, chin in hands, elbows on the table, gazing down at the sad, pale face of the White Lady. By her side Belinda was scribbling away, head down, her tongue sticking out between her lips as she worked.

She had written out the line of Roman numerals and was gradually translating it into Arabic numbers.

'There you go,' she said. 'Done it.'

Holly looked at the list of numbers.

20.15.6.9.14.4.13.5.12.15.15.11.2.5.8.9.14.4.13.5.

'And?' said Holly. 'What does it mean?'

'I don't know,' said Belinda. 'Yet.' She shrugged. 'Perhaps it's the number of paces you take. You know, twenty paces to the right, then fifteen paces to the left. And so on.'

'Starting from where?' asked Holly. 'And which is left and which is right?'

'I don't know. I'm not psychic. Starting from where the White Lady was standing, perhaps?'

'Hmm . . .' Holly looked at the design on the folly. A square with one large rectangle and several smaller rectangles inside it, and a lot of lines criss-crossing around it. 'I don't suppose this could be a plan of the Abbey and its grounds?' she said.

'No,' said Belinda. 'I thought of that. I had a look on a map. It doesn't look anything like it. These numbers, though.' Belinda chewed the end of her pen. 'Perhaps they mean something else? Perhaps you're not supposed to think of them as numbers.'

'What, then?' asked Holly.

'I don't know,' said Belinda.

Tracy was sitting back with her feet up on the table, her violin case across her lap. She had dropped in on them for a few minutes before going to her music lesson. 'They could stand for letters,' she said. 'Twenty would be . . .' She worked it out on her fingers. 'Twenty would be a T.'

Belinda stared at her. 'You'd better be wrong,' she said. 'I'm not having you popping in for five minutes and solving something I've been working on for the last half hour.'

Tracy grinned at her. 'Some of us are naturally brilliant,' she said.

Belinda leaned close over her sheet.

The art room door opened. It was Mr Barnard.

'Hello. What are you girls up to?' he asked.

'We were just doing some work on the *White Lady*,' said Holly. 'We've been up to the Abbey, and we think we've found a couple of clues already.'

'Really?' said Mr Barnard. He walked over to the

table and listened as the three girls fought to be the first to tell him what they had discovered.

'David Taylor, the son of the owner of the Abbey, thinks that if we find out who the White Lady was, we'll be able to find the painting,' said Holly.

'I hope he's right,' said Mr Barnard. 'But how do you plan on – '

'Got it!' yelled Belinda. 'Tracy was right. Look!'

Written on her paper were a series of letters: T.O.F.I.N.D.M.E.L.O.O.K.B.E.H.I.N.D.M.E.

'"To find me look behind me,"' said Belinda. 'It's as clear as day. "To find me look behind me." Arrgh!' She jumped up. 'I've solved it!'

'*I've* solved it, you mean,' said Tracy, leaping to her feet.'

'Look behind what, though?' said Holly.

'Behind the summer-house!' said Tracy.

'Or behind the front,' said Belinda. 'Inside the summer-house.'

Mr Barnard looked at his watch. 'I'm afraid I'm going to have to turf you out of here now,' he said. 'I've got some preparations to do for my next lesson.' He leaned over the table and started to roll the painting up.

'I'll put this safely away,' he said. 'You can come back another time.' He opened a cupboard and fitted the roll on the top shelf. 'There you are,' he said. 'Now you won't have to worry about anyone else interfering with it.'

61

'I'll put my notes with it,' said Belinda. 'I'll only lose them otherwise.'

Mr Barnard closed the cupboard.

'Have you marked my homework yet, sir?' asked Holly. She had changed her mind about the painting of Winifred Bowen-Davies. She had written her essay about the *White Lady*. A lot more than the three hundred words he had asked for.

'Not yet,' said Mr Barnard. 'I've been a bit busy at home lately. But don't worry, I'll have it done by next week.'

They left the art room.

'I've got to go to my music class, now,' said Tracy. 'See you two later.'

'And I've got to go and hand my article for the magazine in to my friend Steffie,' said Holly. She grinned. 'Actually, it's the same as my homework for Mr Barnard, except that I've done Steffie a shorter version.'

She left the other two and made her way down to the library. She had the article in her pocket. She had called it 'The Mystery of the White Lady.' In it she had written down all the details they had discovered about the history of the White Lady, including the search for the stolen painting.

She thought it made very good reading. She hoped Steffie Smith would like it enough not to chop it up the way she'd chopped up the hockey match report.

Steffie took it without a word.

'I'm in time for it to be fitted in, aren't I?' asked Holly.

'Yes,' said Steffie, not even looking up from her word processor.

'Good,' Holly said pointedly. 'I'll look forward to seeing it in the next issue.'

'Probably,' said Steffie.

Holly paused, then decided not to get into a row. She'd have plenty to say if it didn't get in.

Holly, Jamie and Mrs Adams were sitting at the dining table. Food was steaming on the plates. Their father's chair was empty.

'It'll get cold if he doesn't hurry up,' said Mrs Adams. 'I called him twenty minutes ago.'

'You know what he's like when he's working,' said Holly. 'Half the time he doesn't hear you. Shall I go and fetch him?'

'No,' said her mother. 'It's his own fault.'

The door to the dining room flew open. 'What's my own fault?' asked Mr Adams. He came into the room, carrying a brand new, white-wood chair. 'I thought I'd finish this first,' he said with a grin. 'I thought someone might like the privilege of eating their dinner whilst sitting on the first piece of finished furniture from the Adams Workshop.'

'You're getting sawdust all over the place,' said his wife.

'Never mind about that,' he said, circling the table. 'Come along. Up you get.' Mrs Adams stood up and her husband placed the new chair behind her. 'Sit,' he said.

She sat down.

'Well?' he said.

'Very comfortable,' she said, smiling. 'It's lovely. I'm impressed. Now, eat your dinner before it freezes over.'

Later, while Holly and Jamie were doing the washing-up, Holly's mother came into the kitchen.

'I'd like you to take Jamie to the shoe shop after school tomorrow,' she said to Holly. 'He needs a new pair of shoes. Remind me to give you the money in the morning.'

'I can get them on my own,' protested Jamie.

'No, you can't,' said his mother. 'Heaven only knows what you'd come home with if I let you loose in there on your own.'

Holly was no more impressed by the errand than Jamie had been, but she knew better than to argue.

'I know just what I want,' said Jamie as they walked along the street the following day. 'I've seen them.'

'And I know what Mum wants you to have,' said Holly. 'And I doubt if they're the same thing at all.'

'I'm eleven,' said Jamie. 'I don't need a big sister watching over me. Let me go in there and choose on my own, eh? I'll show you what I want before I buy anything.'

'OK,' said Holly. 'I'll wait out here.'

Holly didn't generally enjoy window-shopping, but she wandered along the street, looking in various shops while she waited for Jamie. Knowing him he'd be in there half an hour, driving the assistants crazy before he settled on a pair of shoes he liked.

She crossed a narrow street. Glancing down it she halted, seeing a car she thought she recognised. A small rusty old car with its exhaust-pipe hanging half off. It could only be David Taylor's car. Holly didn't imagine many people in Willow Dale drove about in something as broken-down looking as that.

Holly walked along the side road, looking for David. The shops were shabby and dingy along there, a big change from the bright, clean shops along the front.

She was only a few yards away from the car when she saw David. He came stumbling out of a narrow doorway, as if someone had given him a hefty shove.

Holly's eyes widened in surprise. Standing in the gloomy doorway was the heavy-built man she had seen in the churchyard. The man who had been talking to the man with the eagle on his leather jacket.

'That's not my problem any more,' she heard the man say.

David straightened his rumpled jacket. 'Listen,

65

Mr Owen . . .' He caught sight of Holly and frowned.

Mr Owen followed the line of his eyes, giving Holly a hard look then turning back inside and slamming the door.

David smiled unconvincingly. 'Hello,' he said. 'What are you doing around here?'

'Helping my brother shopping,' said Holly, giving him a puzzled look.

David glanced at the closed door. He seemed distracted and uneasy. 'Can I give you a lift anywhere?' he asked.

'No, thanks,' said Holly. 'Are you OK?'

'Fine,' said David. He waved a dismissive hand. 'Don't worry about old Harry,' he said with another forced smile. 'He's a friend of mine. It's nice to see you again. You never told me your name.'

'Holly.'

'I'll have to remember that,' said David. 'And are you and your friends still planning on coming over on Saturday?'

'I expect so,' said Holly.

'Good. I'll look forward to that.' He smiled. 'If the weather's good we should have a great time with the Red Devil.'

It was clear that David was making conversation to cover his confusion over being seen with Harry Owen.

'Well,' said David. 'I'd better be off.' He jumped into the car. 'I'll catch you later then, Holly.' The engine coughed into life. 'And give my regards to your friends. Tell them I'll be expecting them on Saturday.'

He drove the spluttering car backwards into the main road. Other cars honked their horns as he manoeuvred and trundled off.

It seemed to Holly that David had been more disturbed by his encounter with Harry Owen than he was letting on.

She walked back to the shoe shop. That was the second time she had encountered Harry Owen. She recognised his voice from the conversation she had heard in the churchyard. He was the one who owed the man in the leather jacket the money. Who on earth could they be? And why was David involved?

'Where have you been?' Jamie was outside the shop. 'Come on, hand over the cash. I've found the pair of shoes I want.'

Holly went into the shop with him, but she had other things on her mind than buying shoes.

'Are you Holly Adams?' Holly looked up. She was outside the front of the school, waiting for Belinda and Tracy. It was an older girl that had come up to her, a tall, golden-haired girl with a deep frown on her face.

'Yes.' Holly had seen her around the school, but didn't know who she was. The girl was carrying a copy of the latest issue of the school magazine.

67

'I suppose you think it's fun, raking all this old stuff up again,' said the girl angrily.

Holly was startled. 'Sorry?'

'You wrote that piece on the old painting, didn't you? Steffie Smith told me it was you.'

'Yes, but . . .'

'Why don't you mind your own business? You should never have written that article. And I'm warning you, don't you dare write anything about that painting again, or you'll be in big trouble!' The girl turned and walked rapidly out of the school.

Holly stared, flabbergasted, after her. What on earth had all that been about? The girl had given her no chance to say anything.

Her article for the school magazine had simply been a retelling of the story of the White Lady, with a sentence at the end which read, 'Now that the copy of the painting has been rediscovered, it is thrilling to think that after all these years, the hunt for the missing picture may be beginning again.'

That was innocent enough, surely? Why should anyone take offence at that?

Life in Willow Dale was turning out to be a lot more involved than Holly had ever imagined.

7 A dangerous drive

'From your description I'd have said it was Samantha Tremayne,' said Tracy. 'Except that Samantha Tremayne doesn't behave like that.'

The three girls were on their way to Belinda's house. She had invited them over to meet her horse.

Holly had told them about her encounter with the furious golden-haired girl. Belinda couldn't place her at all, but Tracy thought Holly's description fitted a girl who sang with her in the school choir.

'Samantha's an absolute mouse,' continued Tracy. 'She hardly speaks to anyone. She's real quiet. Always on her own. It's hard to figure why she should have a go at you.'

Holly shrugged. 'Well, she did. And I intend to find out why. I want to know what I did. I hate making enemies.' She pulled a face. 'Except for Steffie Smith, but that's different. She deserves it.'

The three girls came up a hill into a wide road of huge detached houses set back behind tall brick walls. They were in the very best area of Willow

69

Dale, the part of the town where only the richest families could afford to live.

Belinda led them through a side entrance and down into a garden the size of a small park. There was a large chalet-style house and a cluster of low buildings at the far end, and a sweep of open land beyond.

'You never said it was this grand,' said Tracy. She looked at Belinda and shook her head. 'You don't come across like someone who lives in a place like this,' she said.

'Don't I?' said Belinda. 'Good.' She turned and pointed up at the house. 'See that window?' she said. 'That's my room. I'll take you up there later, if you like. Apart from the stables, it's the only other part of the house that's really me.'

They walked the length of the lawn, past trees and flowerbeds.

The long-nosed face of a chestnut thoroughbred appeared above a half-door in one of the brick buildings.

Belinda nuzzled against Meltdown's glossy neck. 'Meltdown,' she crooned, 'these are my friends Holly and Tracy.' She looked at the two girls. 'Isn't he the most perfect thing in the world?'

They spent an hour or so in the stable, helping Belinda clean up. They all came out smelling strongly of horse.

Belinda took them up to the house and into the kitchen, with its Aga cooker and its dark wood beams. Belinda ladled ice cream out of a tub and they were sitting at the table eating when her mother came in. She wore a smart two-piece suit and had a smooth perm with not a hair out of place. Quite a contrast to Belinda.

Belinda introduced her friends.

'I'm glad Belinda has finally started listening to me,' said her mother, 'and started making some friends.'

'I'm just going to show Holly and Tracy my room,' said Belinda.

Her mother looked aghast. 'But it's such a mess,' she said. 'I don't know what your friends will think if they see the state I let you keep it in.'

'They won't mind,' said Belinda.

'No,' said her mother. 'I really would rather you tidied up before showing it to anyone.' She smiled at Holly and Tracy. 'Perhaps you two will have some influence over Belinda. I'm sure I don't. She's got a wardrobe full of lovely clothes up there. But what does she wear all the time? A mouldy old sweatshirt and a pair of jeans that should have been thrown out years ago.'

'Scruffy and proud of it,' murmured Belinda.

'Sorry, dear? What was that?' said her mother.

'Nothing,' said Belinda. 'We'll have some lemonade out in the garden then, if I'm not allowed to take them up to my room.'

The three girls sat on the lawn, drinking lemonade.

71

'That's my mum for you,' Belinda sighed. 'One of you wouldn't fancy doing a swap, would you? Dad's not so bad, though. At least he leaves me alone. When he's here, that is. He spends a lot of time abroad on business.'

'I forgot to mention,' said Holly. 'I met David Taylor. It was a bit odd, actually.' She told her friends about the conversation she had overheard in the churchyard, and about meeting David with the man called Harry Owen. 'David made out it was nothing,' she said. 'But I got the impression he'd had some sort of argument with Harry Owen. I'd like to know what that man does for a living. I'm sure it's something shady.'

Tracy frowned. 'I hope David's not involved in anything like that,' she said. 'Did you hear what was said?'

Holly shook her head. 'Not really,' she said. 'There was mention of something not being Harry Owen's problem any more, but I didn't catch what.'

They pondered for a while over the significance of what Holly had seen. It was certainly disturbing to think of David being involved with a man like Harry Owen, but as Belinda pointed out it was really none of their business. David seemed the sort of boy who could look after himself.

'David asked whether we were still going up to the Abbey on Saturday for a ride in the balloon,' said Holly.

Tracy looked at them. 'We are, aren't we?'

'I'll come with you, if you like,' said Belinda. 'But there's no way in a million years that you'd get me up in that thing. Anyway,' she added, 'I thought we were going to talk about the *White Lady*.' She stretched out on the grass. 'That's much more interesting than whatever David Taylor's up to. It's amazing, isn't it? The Mystery Club hasn't been going for more than a few days, and we're already solving a real mystery.'

'*Trying* to solve a real mystery,' said Tracy.

They spent the rest of the evening talking about their thoughts concerning the strange painting, looking at Kurt's photographs and pondering over the design on the folly.

'I think we should have another look at the real thing tomorrow,' said Belinda. 'These photos are too small, really. First thing tomorrow, OK?'

'Second thing,' said Holly. 'First thing I'm going to try and find Samantha Tremayne and sort out why she was so angry with me.'

Finding Samantha Tremayne the following morning didn't take Holly very long.

'She'll be on her own somewhere with her face stuck in a book,' Tracy had told her. Holly found her sitting on the grass round the back of the tennis courts. She had a large book open in her lap, her head lowered as she read and her face veiled by her long hair.

'Hello,' said Holly.

The girl looked up. 'What do you want?'

'Look,' said Holly. 'I don't know what I've done to upset you, but I want to put it right if I can.'

'It's a bit late for that,' murmured Samantha. 'The harm's been done.'

Holly chewed her lip. 'I'm sorry,' she said. 'Whatever it was.' The girl didn't look up again. Holly looked down at her for a few seconds then gave up and turned to go.

'I don't suppose it occurred to you that there might be people around who'd prefer not to be reminded about all of that?' said Samantha bitterly.

'All of what?' asked Holly.

'The Bastables,' said the girl. 'That story about Roderick Bastable.'

'But it was years ago,' said Holly. 'Who'd mind these days?'

'His great-grandchildren might.'

Holly sat down with a thump. 'You mean there are still some Bastables living around here? I didn't know that. But all the same, why should they mind?'

'If you were brought up with stories of how your great-grandfather threw away the house that you should by rights be living in,' said Samantha vehemently. 'If you were brought up in a poky flat because everything your family had owned had been lost, you might prefer people not to write silly little articles about how funny it all is.'

74

Holly gaped. 'You mean, *you're* a Bastable?'

'My grandmother is Roderick Bastable's daughter,' said Samantha. 'My mother wasn't alive at the time, but she told me how my grandmother was hounded by people asking her about the clues that are supposed to be in that painting.' Samantha slammed her book closed. 'I don't want the whole thing to start again. My gran isn't well. She doesn't need to be reminded of all this. Anyway, you're wasting your time,' added Samantha. 'That painting won't ever be found. People have already searched everywhere. The clues are probably all fake, anyway – the numbers, that meaningless design, the brooch – they're all just nonsense.' Samantha climbed to her feet, her book clasped against her chest. 'I don't want to hear any more about it, right?'

Holly watched sadly as the embittered girl walked away. But something that Samantha had said stuck in Holly's mind. When she had been talking about the clues she had said, the numbers, the design, and the brooch. So that was the third clue. The brooch in the shape of a bird that was pinned to the White Lady's bodice.

Worried by her encounter with Samantha, Holly went off to find Tracy and Belinda.

'I can't believe anyone would still feel like that after all those years,' said Tracy. 'I mean, it's like ancient history, isn't it?'

'All the same,' said Holly. 'I don't like to think

we're upsetting people. I think we should keep our searching fairly low key.'

'Let's go and have another look at the painting,' said Belinda. 'We've got five minutes before registration.'

Mr Barnard wasn't in the art room.

Holly opened the cupboard. The top shelf was empty. The painting and Belinda's notes had been moved.

While they were searching, Mr Kerwood, the deputy head, came into the room.

'What are you girls doing here?' he asked.

'Looking for something that Mr Barnard was keeping for us,' said Holly. 'You don't know where he is, do you?'

'He won't be in today,' said Mr Kerwood. 'He was mugged last night on his way home. He may not be back for a few days.'

'Mugged?' Tracy gasped. 'Was he badly hurt?'

'I don't know the details,' said Mr Kerwood. 'You should be in registration now, shouldn't you?'

The three girls left the art room, worried and subdued.

'I hope he's not too badly hurt,' said Holly. 'Let's see if we can find out more about it.'

It was the talk of the school that morning. By break it had come out that Mr Barnard had been walking from his car to his front door the previous evening when he had been ambushed and robbed. He had fought back and had been beaten up before the attacker had fled with his wallet.

'I don't want to appear unfeeling,' said Belinda at break, 'but I still want to know where he put our painting.'

'We've got Kurt's photos,' said Tracy. 'It's no big deal.'

'But why was it moved?' insisted Belinda. 'And why were all my notes moved as well? Don't you think that's a bit odd?'

'Perhaps Mr Barnard took them home to have a proper look himself,' said Holly. 'Or perhaps he didn't think they were safe enough in that cupboard and put them somewhere else?'

'You're not being very compassionate,' said Tracy. 'I think we should send him a get-well card. To cheer him up.'

'Or we could visit him,' said Belinda. 'That way we could cheer him up *and* ask him where he's put the painting.'

'We could drop in on our way home this afternoon,' said Holly. 'And if he's got the painting with him it'll give us the chance of having a close look at that brooch. Kurt's photos are too small to see it properly.' She nodded thoughtfully. 'Yes,' she said. 'That's a good idea. We'll do that.'

As they were leaving the school that afternoon, the three girls were surprised to see David Taylor's old convertible parked just around the corner. He was sitting at the wheel, looking as if he was waiting for someone.

Tracy tapped on the windscreen and waved at him.

He climbed out. 'Hello,' he said. He smiled at Holly. 'We're always running into each other, aren't we?' He kept looking beyond them. 'It must be fate,' he said.

'A fate worse than death,' murmured Belinda.

Tracy jabbed her in the ribs.

Holly glanced over her shoulder. Samantha Tremayne was standing on the street corner. As she saw Holly and the others she turned and walked rapidly away.

'What are you doing round here?' asked Tracy.

David shrugged. 'Nothing much,' he said, his eyes focused behind them.

'Has your car packed in?' said Belinda.

David looked at them and smiled. 'No, nothing like that. I'm just off, actually. Could I give you a lift anywhere?'

'We were going to visit a teacher who's not well,' said Tracy. 'But it's probably out of your way.'

'I've got plenty of time,' said David. 'On the way you can tell me how you're doing with the clues to the lost painting. Come on, hop in.' He looked at Tracy. 'You can sit in the front. Sorry, I don't know your name.'

'Tracy.'

David looked at Belinda. 'And you're . . .?'

'Winifred,' said Belinda.

'She's called Belinda,' said Tracy, glaring at Belinda. 'You'll have to excuse her sense of humour.'

David laughed. 'OK, then,' he said. 'Tracy in the front by me; Holly and Winifred in the back. You can just about squeeze in, I think.'

'I don't know about this,' said Belinda. 'I think I'd rather walk.'

'Don't be so wet,' said Tracy. 'It'll be great.'

As she was getting into the car, Holly spotted Samantha Tremayne watching them from the far side of the road, a strange expression on her face.

There wasn't a lot of leg-room in the back of the old car, but Belinda and Holly just about managed to squash themselves inside.

With his usual grind of protesting gears, David sent the car clattering down the road.

'This must be the oldest car in Yorkshire,' said Tracy. 'Listen to all the noises it's making.'

'Don't say bad things about it,' said David. 'It might hear you. It's very temperamental.'

'What's that scratching noise?' asked Tracy.

'I don't know. I've been hearing that all afternoon. I think something's loose under the bonnet.' He laughed. 'Don't worry about it. I'm sure nothing will fall off.'

They went over a hump in the road, bouncing about like dice in a cup.

79

'Help!' groaned Belinda. 'Could we go back and collect my stomach?'

They stopped at a traffic light. Belinda leaned over the front seats, giving David directions to Mr Barnard's house.

In the quiet before they started off again, they could all hear the scratching noise that Tracy had mentioned.

'It sounds like it's coming from behind the glove compartment,' said Tracy.

'Loose wires,' said David, changing gears noisily and heading off down the road.

Tracy leaned forwards and opened the compartment's door.

Something black streaked out. Tracy screamed.

'It's a rat!' She kicked out frantically at the dark shape at her feet, grabbing at David in her panic.

There was a shuddering thump as David wrestled with the wheel and the car mounted the pavement.

Brakes howled, and the last thing Holly saw before she flung her arms protectively over her face was a wall rearing up in front of them.

8   The unwelcome visit

The car came to a halt alongside the wall. Tracy hurled the door open and leaped out. The other three were out of the car only a split-second behind her.

Holly saw the black rat streak out from the passenger door and disappear into the long grass by the wall.

Belinda jumped up on to the boot of the car, drawing her feet up.

'Where's it gone?' she shouted. 'Can you see it?'

David ran round the car and kicked through the grass.

'Don't!' shouted Tracy. 'It'll bite you.'

'How did it get in there?' said Holly, keeping well away from the grass.

'I don't know,' said David. 'It could have crawled in, I suppose.'

'I knew I should never have set foot inside this car,' said Belinda. 'Did you see it? It was horrible. I can't stand rats.'

'It's gone now,' said David. He ran his hand

through his hair, frowning at Tracy. 'We could have crashed,' he said.

'Don't blame me,' said Tracy, her voice still shaking. 'I nearly jumped out of my skin.'

'It must have crawled in from underneath,' said David. 'We do have rats sometimes up at the Abbey. You can't kill all of them in a place that big.' He shivered. 'I'm sorry you were frightened,' he said. 'Is everyone all right?'

'I think so,' said Holly. 'But could we get out of here? It might still be lurking about.'

'I'm not getting back in that car,' said Tracy. 'No way! There might be an entire nest of them in there.'

David crawled into the car. He took a spanner and poked around in the glove compartment, then looked round at them.

'There's nothing else in there,' he said. 'Come on. Get back in and I'll drop you off. It's not far now, is it?'

'Give me that spanner, then,' said Tracy. 'I'm not sitting in there without anything to defend myself with.'

Reluctantly, the three girls got back into the car and David started the engine.

'As soon as I get home I'm going to have traps put down,' said David.

'It's weird, though,' said Holly, peering over Tracy's shoulder into the open glove compartment. 'How could it have found its way up there?'

'There must be a hole in the back,' said David.

'I can't see one,' said Tracy.

'Hitch-hiking rats,' said Belinda. 'I've seen every-thing now.'

'Don't joke about it,' said Tracy. 'I've never been so frightened in my life.'

David drove them to the end of the avenue where Mr Barnard lived.

'I hope you're not put off from coming up to the Abbey this weekend,' said David.

'You put those traps out,' said Tracy. 'If I catch sight of a rat at the Abbey, I'll be out of there, right?'

The three girls climbed out of the car and watched as David drove off.

Tracy looked at her friends. 'A rat!' she said. 'Can you believe that? A rat in the glove compartment.' She shook her head. 'It's like a scene out of a horror movie.'

'What number did you say Mr Barnard lived at?' asked Holly. Belinda had got Mr Barnard's address from the school secretary.

'Seventeen,' said Belinda.

They walked along the avenue, counting the house numbers.

'Here we are,' said Holly. She stopped outside an attractive red-brick bungalow with tall evergreen bushes behind its low front wall.

'He lives on his own, you know,' said Belinda. 'My mother is on the parent-teacher's committee. She knows everything that goes on in this town.'

Holly walked up the path. There was no bell, only a small brass knocker.

She rapped the knocker and the three of them waited.

'He must be in,' said Belinda. 'He's hardly likely to be off gallivanting after being beaten up only last night.'

Holly knocked again.

'There doesn't seem to be anyone there,' she said, stepping off the path and peering through the front window. She found herself looking into a long, comfortable room with floor to ceiling windows at the end. Beyond the expanse of glass she could see a patio with a few white plastic chairs arranged on it. Someone was sitting in one of the chairs with his back to her.

'I see him,' said Holly. 'He's in the garden. That's probably why he didn't hear us.' She walked to the side of the house. A low gate barred the alley-way that led round to the back. 'Come on,' she said. 'We can get round this way.'

They walked down the alley.

'Excuse me?' called Holly. 'Hello?' She popped her head around the back corner of the house.

'Mr Barnard? It's only us. We – *oh*!' The man in the chair was staring at her.

But the man in the chair wasn't Mr Barnard.

Before she had time to say anything, Holly was startled by a rustling in the bushes, and Mr Barnard's face appeared over the top of a tall shrub. His face was red and raw as if he had been in a bad fight, one eye half-closed and surrounded by a nasty looking purple bruise.

He frowned. 'Holly Adams? What in heaven's name are you doing here?'

Holly stepped out into the open. Tracy and Belinda were just behind her.

'We came to see how you are,' said Tracy. 'We thought you might need cheering up.'

'It's all round school about you being attacked,' said Holly. 'We thought maybe there was something we could do.'

A look that Holly had registered as shock on Mr Barnard's face changed to one of amazement.

'That's very thoughtful of you,' he said. 'And don't think I don't appreciate it, but . . .' He glanced at the man in the chair. 'I don't really think there's anything you can do. It was a nasty business, but no real damage was done.' He smiled and stepped out of the shrubbery, pulling green gardening gloves off. 'My brother is looking after me. He's . . . visiting me for a while.'

The girls looked over to the other man.

'It was awful that you were attacked,' said Tracy. 'Was much stolen?'

'Nothing irreplaceable,' said Mr Barnard. 'Look, I don't want to seem ungracious, but there really is nothing you girls can do. I really think you ought to be getting off home now.'

He walked towards them, his arms spread to herd them back down the alley.

'It looks worse than it is,' he told them, as they came round to the front of the bungalow. 'I'll probably be back at school in a day or two. It's really nothing for you to worry about.'

'Was your brother hurt?' asked Tracy. 'I noticed he had some marks on his hand.'

Mr Barnard looked sharply at her. 'No,' he said. 'Tom wasn't involved.' He touched his bruised eye. 'I just need some undisturbed rest, that's all. You understand.'

'Of course,' said Holly. 'We didn't mean to disturb you.'

Mr Barnard opened the gate for them. 'It was very kind of you to take the time to come and see me.'

'There was one other thing,' said Belinda. 'We were wondering whether you had the painting of the White Lady here. We couldn't find it in the cupboard where you put it. We could take it back to school for you.'

Mr Barnard shook his head. 'I haven't got it,' he said. 'Are you sure you looked properly?'

'I thought we did,' said Holly. 'I'm sure it wasn't there.'

'I'm afraid I can't help you with that,' said Mr Barnard. 'Someone must have moved it. I dare say it'll turn up. Off you go, girls – and thanks again for coming.'

They walked back down the avenue.

'Odd,' said Belinda.

'What is?' asked Tracy.

'Well, like I told you, my mother knows everything about all the teachers at school. She always told me that Mr Barnard didn't have any relatives. I've certainly never heard of him having a brother.'

'He said his brother was only visiting,' said Holly. 'He probably lives in another part of the country. There's nothing odd about it that I can see.'

'Except that it proves your mother doesn't know everything,' said Tracy.

Belinda nodded. 'True,' she said. 'But that still leaves the question of where the *White Lady* has got to. If Mr Barnard hasn't got it, then who has?'

'We'll have another look tomorrow,' said Tracy. 'Perhaps we did just overlook it. And anyway, we've got the photos, so even if it has vanished, it's no great problem.'

'Except that we can't really see what the brooch looks like from the photos,' said Holly. 'And I don't like the idea of the *White Lady* vanishing like that.'

'We don't know for sure that it has,' said Belinda. 'We didn't have time to look properly. We can have another look tomorrow.'

'And if we don't find it?' asked Holly.

The three girls looked at one another.

'Then we can start getting suspicious about where it's gone,' said Belinda.

Holly arrived at school early the next morning, intending to go straight up to the art room and search thoroughly for the *White Lady*, and for Belinda's missing notes. If they were in there, it shouldn't take more than ten minutes to find them.

She went into the cloakroom to put her bag away.

She opened her locker. There was an envelope at the front. Someone had obviously slid it in under the door.

Puzzled, Holly opened it. Inside was a single folded sheet of paper.

Holly, I'd like to speak to you. It is about the White Lady. *Please don't tell anyone about this.*

The note was signed *Samantha Tremayne*.

9 Peril in the summer-house

Holly slipped Samantha's note into her pocket. What could she want? Samantha had made her feelings about their search for the painting quite clear. Holly didn't like the idea of yet another awkward confrontation with her, but the note didn't read like something written in anger.

Holly ran down the school steps and made her way round to the tennis courts. If Samantha wanted to talk to her in private, Holly guessed that she would be somewhere on her own. The tennis courts seemed the best bet.

It was a chilly morning and the sky was heavy and grey with the threat of rain.

She saw Samantha's solitary figure standing by the high wire fence.

As Holly approached her, she saw Samantha bend down and pick something up. A large carrier bag.

'I got your note,' said Holly.

'I wanted to return this to you,' said Samantha, holding out the bag. 'I shouldn't have taken it. I'm sorry.'

The end of a thick roll of canvas protruded from the bag.

'It's the painting,' said Samantha, her eyes lowered. 'And all your notes.'

Holly looked at her in astonishment.

'I wanted to stop you,' said Samantha. 'I thought that if the painting went missing you might give up.'

'Is it really that important to you?' said Holly.

Samantha shook her head. 'No. Not now. That's why I'm giving it back. It was a stupid thing to do. I realise that now. Will you let me explain?' She looked at Holly and gave her a frail smile. 'It's my gran, you see. She's really very ill.'

'Yes,' Holly said softly. 'You told me. I'm sorry.'

'She's in a nursing home,' said Samantha. 'I visit her as often as I can. I saw her last night. She could see I was upset. I've never been any good at hiding my feelings from my gran. We've always been very close.'

Holly waited for Samantha to continue.

'She wouldn't let me go until I'd told her what was wrong,' said Samantha.

'Was she very upset?' asked Holly.

'No. That's what was so strange. She wasn't upset at all. She said it was about time someone finally found where that painting had been hidden. We had a really long talk about it.' Samantha lapsed into silence.

'Is that why you're giving the painting back?'

asked Holly. 'Because your gran doesn't mind us looking for the original?'

'Partly,' said Samantha. 'But there's more. Something even I didn't know about until last night.' She felt in her jacket pocket and drew out a small wad of tissue. 'She gave me this. She said I was to show it to you.'

Very delicately Samantha unwrapped the tissues. Sitting gleaming black and white in her hand was a brooch. An enamel brooch in the shape of a bird. 'It's a magpie,' said Samantha. 'This is one of an identical pair.'

'It's similar to the brooch in the painting, isn't it?' said Holly.

'Not *similar*,' said Samantha. 'My gran told me that this is the actual brooch in the painting. There's a story behind it. A story that she never told anyone up to now. Not even my mother.'

'You don't have to tell me if it's private,' said Holly.

'I want to tell you. Gran wants me to tell you. You see, there's something about the White Lady that only my gran knew, something that she told me about last night. It's the story behind the brooch that might help you.'

Samantha took a deep breath. 'You see, the White Lady was tutor to Hugo Bastable's children. She worked for him at the Abbey. She even lived there for a time. Which was how it happened.'

'How what happened?' asked Holly.

91

'They fell in love. Hugo and the White Lady fell in love with each other. Apparently Hugo was prepared to give up everything to be with her. His family, the Abbey – everything. But she wouldn't let him. She told him she was going away. He did the portrait of her as a sort of keepsake, so at least he'd have something to remember her by. She gave him one of the pair of magpie brooches on the day she left. My gran told me that the brooch wasn't in the original painting – it was put in the copy as a clue.'

'Does your gran know who the White Lady was?' asked Holly gently.

Samantha shook her head. 'No one knows that. My gran told me that Hugo destroyed all records of the White Lady after she left the Abbey. The only thing he kept was the portrait of her.' Samantha looked up at Holly and smiled sadly. 'Hugo kept her identity secret for years. But after his wife died, he told his son.' Samantha looked at Holly. 'Roderick was the only person he told. And it was Roderick who told the story to his daughter – my gran. He was in the prison hospital. He was dying, you see, and he wanted my gran to be able to find the stolen painting so that his debts could be paid off. They were never left alone, so Roderick couldn't tell her where the painting was hidden. He gave her this brooch and told her to find the *White Lady*. Apparently those were the last words he ever spoke to her, "Find the *White Lady*".'

Holly was thoughtful. 'But she must have died a long time ago,' she said. 'It's a terribly sad story, but I don't see how it can help us find the stolen painting.'

'My gran thinks that Hugo told Roderick who the White Lady was, and that Roderick hid the painting with her,' said Samantha. 'That would explain what he meant by "find the White Lady." She thinks that if you can find out who the White Lady was, it might lead you to the painting.'

Samantha wrapped the brooch again and slid it back into her pocket. 'I'm sorry for the way I behaved yesterday,' she said. 'And I'm sorry I took the painting. I'm so tired these days that I hardly know what I'm doing half the time. It's the nursing home fees, you see. My gran doesn't have any money, and my mother can't pay for it all, so I work three nights a week and at weekends to help out.'

'Thanks for telling me all this,' said Holly. 'I'm sure it will help us find the painting. Tell your gran we'll do everything we can.'

Samantha smiled. 'I shall,' she said. 'I'm sure it'll make her feel better if the painting is found.'

Holly smiled. 'We'll find it,' she said. 'I'm sure we will now.'

The rain was falling steadily out of the grey sky. Holly stood holding an umbrella over Tracy's mother as she carried the last box up the path to the terraced house where she and Tracy lived.

'Not very good weather for this sort of thing is it?'
Mrs Foster said to the three friends. 'But thanks for
helping. I'd have got soaked otherwise. How about
a cup of tea and some sandwiches as a reward?'

Holly, Tracy and Belinda had been helping
Mrs Foster collect toys and games in the neighbourhood. The nursery that Tracy's mother ran
was always in need of more things for the children
to play with, and the leaflets she had posted in local
shops had drawn a good response.

The hallway was piled with boxes and carrier
bags. Mrs Foster closed the front door and dumped
the box on the heap.

'People are very kind,' she said. 'But it's exhaus-
ting work collecting door to door. Let's go through
into the kitchen and have a breather.'

'We could help you sort through it all,' said
Holly.

'Not now,' said Tracy's mother. 'I'm not doing
another thing until tomorrow.' She smiled. 'I think
we've done enough for one day, don't you?'

The kitchen was small and cheerful, the walls
covered with big, colourful paintings done by the
children Mrs Foster looked after.

Tracy made some sandwiches while they waited
for the kettle to boil. A flurry of rain pattered
against the window.

'Right,' said her mother. 'I'm off for my nap,
now.' She took her cup of tea and left them to eat
the sandwiches.

'She always has a quick sleep about this time,' explained Tracy. 'Half an hour on the couch and she's as good as new. Let's go up to my room.'

Tracy's bedroom was immaculate. Belinda stared round at the neat shelves and spotless carpet.

'Is it like this all the time?' she asked. 'It makes my room look like a jumble sale.'

'It's easier to find things if you keep it tidy,' said Tracy. She pulled some large cushions out from under the bed and they sat down.

'Shall we have another think about the White Lady?' suggested Holly. She had already told them about her meeting with Samantha and all the new information she had been given.

'Samantha's gran's story is really helpful,' said Tracy. 'But the White Lady would have gotten old and died *years* ago. If no one knows who she was, how are we supposed to find out anything about her?'

'It's odd,' said Holly. 'That brooch looked familiar, somehow. But I can't think why.'

'Did you notice that there were sculptures of birds on the edges of the roof on the summer-house?' said Tracy. 'You can't really see them in the photos of the painting, but I noticed them the other day at the Abbey. A bird on each corner of the roof.'

'She's done it again,' said Belinda. 'Tracy Foster, I hate you.'

'What have I done now?' asked Tracy

'The summer-house,' breathed Holly. 'And it says, "To find me look behind me."'

'I didn't say the birds were magpies,' said Tracy. 'They might be anything.'

'They're not going to be ostriches, are they?' said Belinda. 'I'll bet you anything you like that they're magpies. Well, there's only one way to find out. We'll have to go back there.'

'We can't this evening,' said Tracy. 'It'll be closed by now. And I've promised to babysit tomorrow. We're due to go there on Saturday anyway for a ride in David's balloon. We can look then.'

'I don't really fancy going over there in this weather anyway,' said Holly, looking out of the bedroom window at the falling sheets of rain. 'If the painting's hidden in the summer-house it won't be going anywhere for a day or two, will it?'

'I hope this rain goes away by Saturday,' said Tracy. 'I can't see David taking us up in his balloon in the middle of a storm.'

'You won't be seeing him taking me up in it whether it's raining or not,' said Belinda.

Tracy and Holly exchanged a secret grin. Belinda might not think she was going up in the Red Devil, but her two friends had other ideas.

The weather didn't improve over the next couple of days. In fact it got worse. Occasional bright spots when the clouds seemed to be thinning were always followed by another great dark bank that sent rain tumbling down over the hills.

By Saturday it seemed as if every raincloud in the county had come to roost over Willow Dale. Lightning ricocheted off the hills and thunder rumbled and roared.

Belinda was already at the bus stop when Holly arrived.

'Tracy's chances of a balloon ride in this lot are about zero,' she said. 'We should have called it off.'

'We can still have a look at the summer-house,' said Holly. 'I can't bear to have to wait any longer.'

Tracy came running up, half hidden by a huge umbrella with coloured panels. 'Are we catching a bus, or shall we just swim there?' she said.

It wasn't a long wait for the bus. It came swishing through the rain and they tumbled on board, glad to get out of the cold.

The bus dropped them opposite the long gravel lane. It ran with water as they picked their way carefully down to the gates. The gates to the grounds of Woodfree Abbey were open as usual, but the car park was a deserted sea of rain-pocked water.

The sky blazed white and a crash of thunder shook the air.

'It's right overhead,' said Holly as the reverberations died away and the gloom returned.

They slithered their way up to the house. There wasn't a single other person in sight.

They stood looking up at the roof of the summer-house. Rain was cascading down from the broken guttering. As Tracy had said, a small stone bird sat at each corner of the roof.

'Well?' said Belinda. 'Are they magpies? My glasses are too wet for me to see.'

'They are!' said Holly. 'Magpies! I'm certain of it.'

'So?' said Tracy. 'Do we go inside?' She looked at the boarded-up windows and the padlocked door. 'Can we get inside?'

They made their way round to the back of the summer-house. The windows round there were also sealed by boards, except that on one window the nails holding the boards had fallen out. It hung slightly askew.

Tracy pulled at the board and it came loose. She squeezed herself into the gap.

'Can you see anything?' asked Holly.

'Not much,' said Tracy. 'It's very dark in there, but . . .' They heard a dry, grating sound. 'I've done it,' she said.

They watched as her feet lifted out of the mud and disappeared.

'Tracy?'

There were noises from inside, then Tracy's voice. 'I'm in,' she called. 'Come on. You can climb through. It's easy.'

Tracy had managed to heave the window open. Holly followed her through. Dubiously Belinda looked at the gap. Then she looked up at the teeming rain. 'Wait for me,' she said.

They stood dripping in a dark and dusty room. They rested their umbrellas against the wall. A wet patch spread on the grimy floor. A few pieces of furniture stood about, shrouded in dust-sheets. Wallpaper was peeling from the stained walls. There was an overpowering smell of rot.

'Not very thrilling, is it?' said Belinda. Old floorboards creaked as she walked about, lifting corners of the sheets. 'What do you think?'

'Well, I didn't expect it to be hanging on the wall,' said Holly. 'We've got to search.'

It was only a small building, divided into three rooms.

'What about here?' said Holly. In the third room was a large pile of rolled up carpets.

'I'm not touching them,' said Belinda. 'They stink!'

'We've got to search properly,' said Holly, hauling at one of the carpets. It crumbled unpleasantly in her hands.

A pair of step-ladders lay against one wall.

'Look!' said Tracy, pointing at the ceiling. They looked up at a square trap-door. 'That must be the way into the loft,' she said.

'If you think for one minute . . .' began Belinda. An enormous clap of thunder drowned her out.

Holly and Tracy dragged the step-ladders out under the trap-door and pulled them upright.

'Holly,' said Belinda, 'be sensible.'

'But that's the exact place to hide something,' said Holly. 'We've got to look up there.'

Tracy climbed the ladder and pushed at the trap. 'I can't . . . quite . . . Oh!' The trap-door opened so suddenly that she nearly lost her balance.

'Careful!' called Holly. Belinda had her hands over her eyes.

'It's OK,' said Tracy. The other two watched as she clambered up and out of sight.

'What's it like?' shouted Holly.

'Dark,' came Tracy's voice. 'And extremely dirty.'

Holly followed her up the ladder.

The smell of rotting wood was very strong as Holly came up through the trap-door into the gloom. Slivers of light showed through the roof. She could see Tracy's crouching shape moving about.

Something pushed Holly from beneath. 'Come on,' said Belinda. 'I want a look, too.'

Holly crawled into the roof space and made room for Belinda to come up after her.

'Found anything?'

'I don't think there's anything up here,' said Tracy. 'I'm getting filthy.'

Holly crawled out of the way as Belinda pulled herself up.

'Be very careful,' warned Tracy. 'The floor doesn't feel too safe.'

'We need a torch,' said Belinda. 'I can't see a thing.' She reached up and, using Holly's shoulder, clambered to her feet. 'Ow!'

'What?'

'I've banged my head on a beam,' said Belinda.

'Keep on all fours,' said Tracy.

'I'm all right,' said Belinda.

The light flared suddenly through the cracks and a clap of thunder shook the building.

Then there was another sound. An ominous creaking from the floor.

'Belinda!' exclaimed Tracy. 'Be careful, will you?'

'It's not me,' said Belinda. 'It's – '

The creaking turned into the grinding groan of cracking wood. There was a terrible rush of noise, and as Holly and Tracy watched helplessly, Belinda fell with a scream through the collapsing floor.

10 The trespasser

'Belinda!' Holly tried to grab at her friend as she fell. She grasped an edge of Belinda's coat but it was wrenched out of her hand.

'Oh, my Lord!' gasped Tracy. A choking cloud of dust billowed up around them.

There was a dull thud.

'Belinda?' coughed Holly, trying to see down through the ragged hole without falling herself. 'Are you OK?'

There was no sound from below.

'Quick!' said Tracy. 'Let's get down there.'

It wasn't easy, climbing backwards on to the step-ladders, especially knowing what they might find in the room beneath.

Belinda was sitting up in the middle of the pile of carpets, her coat speckled with woodchips and her face grey with dirt. She coughed, picking wood splinters out of her hair.

'Are you OK?' asked Holly.

'Can you see my glasses?' asked Belinda.

'Never mind your glasses,' said Holly. 'Have you hurt yourself?'

Belinda pulled the collar of her coat down from around her ears. 'I don't think so,' she said. She clambered down off the heap. 'Ouch,' she said.

Holly picked up her glasses and handed them to her.

'Good,' said Belinda, putting them on. 'At least they're not broken.' She looked up at the hole. 'And for my next trick,' she said, 'I shall go over Niagara Falls in a soup tureen.'

'You are a clumsy great lump,' said Tracy. 'You scared the life out of me.'

'Sorry,' said Belinda. 'Ow! I hurt all over. Whose stupid idea was this anyway?'

'I think we'd better get out of here,' said Holly.

'What about the damage?' asked Tracy.

They all looked up at the ceiling. There was an enormous hole.

'Do you think anyone will notice?' said Belinda.

'I think they might,' said Holly. 'Perhaps we should go and confess.'

'We should go and tell David, at least,' said Tracy.

They eased themselves out through the window. The rain was still pelting down, but the darkly thunderous clouds had drifted away. The worst of the storm seemed to be over.

They put up their umbrellas and sploshed over towards the house.

'I hope David will be sympathetic,' said Holly. 'I don't fancy being yelled at.'

'I'm sure he will be,' said Tracy.

They made their way round to the front of the house.

The woman sitting at the paydesk stared at them in astonishment. 'You're very brave, coming out in weather like this,' she said. She eyed Belinda's coat. 'What have you been up to?'

'Just having fun,' said Belinda. 'You know. Like people do when it's wet out.'

'Is David Taylor around?' asked Tracy.

'Oh, I see,' she said. 'You're friends of David, are you? Wait there, then. I'll see if I can locate him for you. Try not to drip on the carpet, please. It's Georgian.'

They stepped back into the lobby.

Five minutes later David appeared.

'You're wet,' he said, smiling.

'Never!' said Belinda. 'How did that happen?'

David laughed. 'Sorry,' he said. 'Silly thing to say. I'm afraid there's no chance of getting the balloon up in this,' he said. 'But I can run to a cup of coffee, if you'd like something to drink. You look as if you could do with warming up.'

'If it's no trouble,' said Tracy.

'Of course not. I'd usually be helping to show people around at this time of day. But as you can see, we're not exactly swarming with visitors. Come on. I'll show you some of the places the tourists never get to see.'

They left their wet coats and umbrellas at the

door and he took them through the house. Room after room was filled with gorgeous old furniture. There were cabinets laden with shining silverware and four-poster beds with heavy, patterned curtains. The wood-panelled corridors were lined with portraits.

'This is where we live,' he told them, leading them up a staircase and through an oak-panelled door. 'My father isn't here at the moment. I more or less have the place to myself most of the time.'

'You're actually in charge of everything, are you?' asked Holly.

'Not really. We have a company that deals with the visitors and the upkeep and everything. I just help out by showing people around. Sit down and make yourselves comfortable. I'll only be a minute.'

He left them in a sumptuous room with dark red flock wallpaper and large couches.

'This is OK, isn't it?' said Tracy, bouncing on one of the couches.

David came back carrying a tray.

'Aha!' said Belinda, grinning. 'The famous cream scones.'

Tracy laughed. 'You've made her day now,' she said.

'We've got a bit of a confession to make,' said Holly.

'That sounds interesting,' said David. 'What have you done?'

105

Holly told him about their troubles in the summer-house, and about the brooch that Samantha had shown her. The third clue.

He was frowning and thoughtful as she finished.

'We're terribly sorry about the damage,' said Holly.

'Don't worry about that,' he said. 'The old place ought to have been demolished years ago.' He shook his head. 'The whole lot might have come crashing down around your ears, though. I wish you'd mentioned it to me before you decided to go in there.'

'We should have done,' said Tracy. 'Sorry.'

'I don't mind you searching,' said David. 'But I could have saved you the bother. That place has been turned inside out over the years.' He spread his hands. 'If someone had hidden a postage stamp in there it would have been found. People have even had the floorboards up.'

'And we were so sure,' said Holly. 'It looks like we're back to square one again. But there's still Samantha's brooch, isn't there? You didn't know about that before now, did you?'

'No,' said David, a strangely thoughtful expression on his face. 'I didn't know anything about that.' He sat staring at the carpet.

'Is there something wrong?' asked Holly.

David looked up and shook his head. 'No,' he said. 'I don't suppose so.' He smiled. 'No. It's nothing. Nothing important. But I don't think you'll have any luck by searching for magpies. Look.' He

106

pointed to the carved architrave over the door. 'See?'

In amongst the intricate scrollwork the girls saw a pair of beautifully sculpted magpies.

'They're all over the place, if you look,' said David. 'The magpie was the emblem of the Bastable family. Old Hugo Bastable had them carved all over the house.'

'That must be why the White Lady sent him a magpie brooch,' said Holly.

'Yes. The mysterious White Lady,' said David. 'Wouldn't it be something if we could find out who she was? Then we could find the painting and . . .' He looked up, as if suddenly realising he was thinking aloud.

'Might there still be some reference to her here?' asked Holly. 'Something that Hugo didn't destroy?'

David shrugged. 'I suppose we could look,' he said. 'I'll tell you what, they'll be closing up in a little while. How about if the four of us have a rummage around? Perhaps between us we'll spot something that no one's ever noticed before. And then I'll drive you home.'

'I'd rather get the bus, if you don't mind,' said Belinda. 'Unless you're certain that all the rats have been caught.'

David frowned. 'Oh, yes,' he said. 'The rat.'

'Have you caught any others?' asked Tracy.

'No,' said David. 'Not yet. I'll just go and tell them they can close up a bit early. Shan't be long.'

David was back within ten minutes. 'All done,' he said. 'We've got the whole place to ourselves now. Come on, let's see if we can find out anything about that White Lady.'

It was fascinating to be given the run of the wonderful old house. David knew a lot of the history and told them stories as they wandered through the rooms.

'This is where the original of the *White Lady* used to hang,' he told them, taking them into a room in the east wing.

Belinda was looking out of the window. 'Someone's getting wet,' she said.

David looked over her shoulder. A little way in the distance they could dimly see a figure running through the gloom of the early evening.

'That's funny,' said David. 'There shouldn't be anyone in the grounds now. The gates were locked a couple of hours ago.'

'Perhaps someone was sheltering from the rain and got themselves locked in,' said Tracy.

'They won't be able to get out then,' said David. 'I'd better go and check.'

Holly looked at her watch. 'Crumbs,' she said. 'Look at the time.'

The hours had flown by whilst they had been looking around the house. It was mid-evening already.

'I really ought to be going,' she told David. 'My parents will be expecting me home soon.'

'I've shown you just about everything anyway,' said David. 'I'll come down to the gates and unlock them for you. We'll pick that poor lost soul up on the way. He won't get out otherwise. The walls around this place are eight feet high.'

They went to the front and put their coats on. The rain had lost most of its power, falling now as a fine drizzle which the wind whipped into their eyes.

'Can you see him anywhere?' asked David as they made their way down to the gates. 'He ought to be around here somewhere if he's trying to get out.'

'There!' cried Tracy. 'Look. There he is.'

They saw a movement amongst the trees over to the right of the gates. It was only a dim shadow, moving stealthily through the trees.

'Hey!' shouted David. 'You there!'

The figure darted out of sight.

'I don't like this,' said David. 'Stay here, I'm going to go and see what he's up to.'

David ran into the trees.

'Come on,' said Tracy. 'We might be able to help.' She ran after David.

'You're mad,' shouted Belinda. 'Come back here. He could be anyone!'

'We can't leave her to it,' said Holly. The two of them ran after Tracy.

Beneath the trees the rain fell in slow, heavy drops. It was treacherous underfoot, and more than once Holly nearly fell. It was difficult to see very much in the twilight that lay beneath the spreading branches. Tracy had sprinted out of sight. They could still hear David's voice.

'We'll break our necks,' cried Belinda, skidding on a slippery knee of tree root.

They heard Tracy give a yell.

Holly darted around a broad tree-trunk and fell slithering backwards as a looming shape buffeted against her.

It was the man. She had run into his back. She was sent sliding away from him. She collided with Belinda and they both tumbled into the mud.

As she clambered to her feet, Holly saw Tracy running after the fleeing figure.

He was running for the gates. Even in the gathering darkness, Holly could see the eagle printed on the back of his leather jacket.

By the time Tracy came sprinting out of the trees, the man was already climbing the high wrought-iron gates. There was no sign or sound of David.

Tracy stood clinging to the gates, watching as the man ran up the long slope to the road. Holly raced up behind her.

'Where's David?' gasped Tracy. 'He'll get away if we don't get these gates open.'

Holly looked round. Belinda was just coming out of the trees, but there was still no sign of David.

Tracy rattled the gates in frustration. The running man was already well up the slope. There seemed little chance of catching him now.

But where was David?

11   David Taylor's secret

'Perhaps David's hurt,' said Tracy anxiously, scanning the trees for some sign of him.

'What about the man?' said Belinda, gesturing up the slope beyond the gates. The mysterious interloper could no longer be seen.

'You chase him, if you want to,' said Tracy. 'I'm going to find David.' She ran back into the trees, calling his name.

Belinda shook her head, leaning against the gates. 'I can't run any more,' she said. 'I'm exhausted.'

Holly trotted after Tracy.

'Be careful,' called Belinda.

Holly gave her a reassuring wave.

She found them almost immediately. David was crouched on the ground with his back to a tree. He was holding a handkerchief to his face. A handkerchief with blood on it. Tracy was leaning over him.

'Thank heavens!' said Holly. 'Did he hurt you badly?'

David looked up at her. 'He didn't hurt me at all,' he said. 'I didn't get anywhere near him. I slipped and hit my face on a stone or something.' He dabbed at his bleeding nose.

He stood up, leaning on Tracy's shoulder.

'Who do you think he was?' asked Tracy.

'I don't know,' said David.

'I do,' said Holly. 'His name is Barney. At least, that's what Harry Owen called him.'

David stared at her. 'What are you talking about?'

Holly told David about the conversation she had heard between Harry Owen and the man he called Barney.

'I wouldn't have anything to do with that Owen man, if I were you,' said Holly. 'I don't think he's a very pleasant person.'

David's eyes narrowed. 'And I'd keep my nose out of other people's business, if I were you,' he snapped. 'You don't know what you're talking about.'

'David,' said Tracy. 'There's no need to get angry.'

'I think there is,' said David. 'Holly obviously thinks I'm involved in something criminal.' He glared at Holly. 'If you must know,' he said, 'I bought my car from Harry Owen. I went to see him to complain about the fact that it's falling to pieces. That's all that was going on when you saw us.'

'Oh!' Holly was taken aback. 'I didn't realise.'

'No, you didn't. If I were you, I'd get my facts straight before I went around offering advice.'

Holly's face reddened. 'I didn't mean any harm,' she said. 'And that was the man I saw with Harry Owen, whatever you say.'

'Did you see his face?' asked David.

'No,' admitted Holly. 'But it was the same jacket. I'm sure of that.'

'Do you seriously think that this Barney, or whatever you called him, is the only man in the world with an eagle printed on the back of his leather jacket?' said David. 'If you ask me, you're letting your imagination run away with you.'

'Don't be so patronising,' said Holly. 'I'm not stupid.'

That's a matter of opinion,' David said harshly.

'Now look here . . .' began Holly, becoming angry in her turn.

'Please, you two, don't argue,' said Tracy. She looked at David. 'Holly wasn't suggesting you were involved in anything wrong. But if you're in some kind of trouble, perhaps we could help?'

'I'm not in trouble,' said David. 'I don't need any help.'

Nothing else was said as they walked down to the gates.

'You're OK, are you?' said Belinda. She looked at the three of them. 'Is something wrong?'

David unlocked the gates.

'What's going on?' asked Belinda, as the three girls started up the hill.

'Nothing,' snapped Holly.

113

Belinda looked enquiringly at Tracy. Tracy shook her head.

They caught the bus and journeyed home to Willow Dale in silence.

'What is it?' asked Belinda eventually.

'He thinks I'm stupid,' murmured Holly. 'I don't want to talk about it.'

'Are you sure it was the same man?' asked Tracy.

'What man?' asked Belinda. 'Will someone tell me what's going on here?'

'Holly thinks it was the man she saw with Harry Owen,' said Tracy.

'I don't *think* it was,' said Holly. 'I'm *sure* it was. And I'm pretty sure David knows it was as well.'

'What makes you say that?' asked Tracy.

'Didn't you hear what David said?' asked Holly. 'He mentioned the eagle printed on the back of the man's jacket. But he said he didn't get anywhere near the man. So how did he know he was wearing a leather jacket with an eagle on the back? I didn't tell him. I never mentioned the eagle.'

'Then he must have seen it,' said Tracy. 'I think we should go back and talk to him when you've both calmed down.'

The rest of the journey home took place in an uneasy silence.

That night Holly didn't sleep very well. She couldn't get the thought out of her mind that David hadn't been telling the truth about his dealings with Harry Owen. Would he really have reacted that angrily if all he had done was to buy a car from Harry Owen?

But if there was more to it, what on earth could David be involved in?

There was at least one piece of good news in school on Monday morning. Mr Barnard was back.

Holly, walking thoughtfully across the teachers' car park, saw him getting out of his car. She went over to him.

His face was still bruised, but he smiled at her and nodded at a pile of exercise books under his arm.

'Every cloud has a silver lining,' he said. 'At least my forced absence gave me time to mark some homework.'

'Did you like my essay on the White Lady?' asked Holly, walking to the school building with him.

'I would have preferred more about the painting itself, and less of the legend behind it,' said Mr Barnard. 'It wasn't meant to be a history essay, was it?'

'But you said I should write about why I liked it,' said Holly. 'And it was the story behind it that I liked.'

Mr Barnard laughed, gently rubbing his sore eye with the edge of his hand. 'You've got me there,' he said. 'By the way, did you find the copy?'

'Oh, yes,' said Holly. 'It wasn't missing. Someone had borrowed it. It's back in your cupboard again. How are you feeling?'

115

'Much better,' said Mr Barnard.

'Have the police got anywhere with their investigations?' asked Holly.

Mr Barnard looked sharply at her. 'What do you mean?' he said. 'What investigations?'

'Into whoever it was that mugged you,' explained Holly.

An anxious look passed across Mr Barnard's face. 'Oh, that,' he said. 'No, I don't suppose there's much chance of him being found.'

'Did you manage to give them a good description of him?'

'To be honest with you, Holly, I hardly saw the man. He came up behind me. It was all over before I knew what was happening. But talking about investigations, how are you getting on with your search for the White Lady?'

Holly told him about the magpie brooch. She didn't mention their fruitless search of the summerhouse, or Samantha Tremayne's part in it all. She didn't think Samantha would want her story broadcast all over the school.

'You seem to be doing very well,' said Mr Barnard. 'You keep this up, and I wouldn't be a bit surprised if you come up with the goods.'

'Do you really think so?' said Holly.

'Why not?' said Mr Barnard. 'That painting is certainly hidden somewhere.' They walked into the hall. The portrait of Winifred Bowen-Davies stared sternly down at them. 'I'd better go and report to Miss Horswell,' said Mr Barnard. He smiled at Holly. 'You keep searching,' he said.

'The funny thing is,' said Holly, when she met up with Tracy and Belinda at break, 'Mr Barnard told me he hadn't been able to give the police a description of the man who mugged him because he was attacked from behind.'

'What's so funny about that?' asked Belinda. 'There's nothing particularly funny that I can see about having your face bashed in.'

'But that's the whole point,' said Holly. 'How do you get your face in that sort of mess if you're attacked from behind?'

'He was probably knocked over,' said Tracy. 'He probably hit his face on the pavement or something as he fell.'

'I suppose so,' said Holly. 'But it looked like the sort of damage you'd get from a fist. From being punched in the face. It just seems strange to me that he didn't see the man.'

'No wonder you wanted to start up a mystery club,' said Belinda. 'You're seeing mysteries everywhere. First David's tangled up with arch-criminals, and now Mr Barnard's under suspicion. Isn't the White Lady enough to keep your brain occupied?'

Holly smiled. 'I know,' she said. 'I've got an overactive imagination.'

'Speaking of David,' said Tracy. 'I was thinking of going up to the Abbey this afternoon . . . just

117

to see how he is. Anyone want to come with me?'

Holly shook her head. 'No, thanks,' she said. 'I'd rather keep away from David for the time being.'

'You're not still annoyed, are you?' said Tracy. 'Can't you just forget what he said? After all, he is helping us search for the *White Lady*. You never know what else we might discover up there.'

'I'm busy this afternoon,' said Holly. 'You and Belinda go up there if you want to. If you find out anything, you can let me know in the morning.'

Holly wasn't being completely truthful about her evening. Apart from some homework, she didn't really have much to do at all.

She had dinner with her parents. Jamie was out at his friend Philip's house. Philip's computer games seemed to draw boys from all over the neighbourhood. Holly hardly ever saw her brother these days.

Her father was reading the *Express*, the local newspaper run by Kurt Welford's father.

'This is interesting,' he said. 'There's an article in here about an exhibition at the library. A display of old photographs of how Willow Dale looked at the turn of the century. We could go along and have a look at that at some stage, couldn't we? I should think that would be interesting. Old photos can be fascinating.'

Later that evening Holly was sitting in her bedroom, gazing out over the garden. Perhaps she ought to have gone up to the Abbey to make her peace with David. After all, it wasn't really her business what he did with Harry Owen. And Owen did look the sort that might con someone into buying a broken-down car. But that still didn't explain his behaviour over the trespasser. The mysterious Barney. What had he been doing at the Abbey?

Holly sighed. Was her imagination running away with her?

She decided to cheer herself up by writing a long letter to Miranda. Her other close friend from London, Peter Hamilton, was car-mad. She would write to him as well, and tell him about David's old banger of a car. The story of the rat in the glove compartment would amuse him no end.

She was just sealing her two letters when her bedroom door burst open.

'I've borrowed Devil Riders from Philip,' said Jamie. 'Have a game with me, Holly?'

'I don't like computer games,' said Holly.

'But it needs two players,' pleaded Jamie. 'I can't play on my own. Come on, Holly. Just this once.'

'Oh, all right, then. But only a quick game,' said Holly. An hour or so with Jamie, playing one of his games, might take her mind off her problems.

Jamie's room echoed to the zap and screech as the Devil Riders zoomed across the screen, blasting the alien vampires with the ray guns mounted on their motorbikes.

It was so loud that she didn't hear the telephone.

119

The first thing she knew about her phone call was when her father popped his head around the door.

'Tracy's on the phone for you,' he told her.

Holly went downstairs.

'You should be careful with those computer games,' said her father. 'They can be addictive, you know.'

'So I've noticed,' said Holly. 'There are still another ten million vampires to slaughter before the planet is safe.' She grinned. 'I didn't think I'd like computer games, but this one's quite fun.'

Her father left her to speak on the telephone.

'Holly? Is that you?' It was Tracy's voice. 'Listen, I've got something really weird to tell you.'

'What's happened?' asked Holly.

'We went up to the Abbey. I've only just this minute got back home,' said Tracy. 'Listen, Holly. You're never going to believe who was up there with David. Not just *with* him, but holding hands with him – like she's his girlfriend, or something.'

'Who?' asked Holly.

'Samantha Tremayne,' said Tracy. 'Samantha Tremayne was up at the Abbey with David – and we saw them. Holly, we saw them kissing each other.'

'Are you sure?' said Holly in surprise. 'They never mentioned they knew each other.'

'They know each other, all right,' said Tracy. 'From what Belinda and I saw, I'd say they know each other very well indeed.'

12 Real detective work

Holly's priority the next morning was to find Samantha. Her initial astonishment at Tracy's revelation had given way to a feeling of annoyance. What sort of game was Samantha playing with her? Why hadn't she told her she was friends with David Taylor right from the start? She had spoken as if her family didn't like the Taylors, and all the time it seemed as if she was David's girlfriend. Why hadn't David said anything when they had told him about the brooch?

A couple of other things fell into place. David waiting outside the school that afternoon when he had given them a lift. Samantha coming round the corner, then walking off when she saw them with him. The strange look she had given them as they had driven off. David must have been waiting for Samantha. So why was nothing said? What was the big secret? Holly was determined to get to the bottom of it.

She found a few of Samantha's classmates, but no one had seen her. She hunted around the school.

Then, in the library, Holly saw a familiar head of golden hair bowed over a book.

Samantha looked up at her.

'Hello, Holly,' she said, smiling.

'I don't like people trying to make a fool of me,' said Holly, not angrily but determinedly. 'I want to know what you think you're up to with David Taylor.'

Samantha stared at her. 'What do you mean?'

'You were seen,' said Holly. 'With David. At Woodfree Abbey. Are you and David playing some sort of game with us? Feeding us clues about the *White Lady* to make fun of us? What was the idea? Were we supposed to run around like idiots while you had a good laugh at our expense? Was that it?'

'No. Of course not,' said Samantha. 'It was nothing like that. Honestly, Holly, it's not like that at all. You don't understand.'

'Then explain it to me.' She sat down opposite Samantha. 'I want to know, Samantha. I'm not leaving here until you tell me the truth.'

'I've been seeing David secretly for six months,' said Samantha softly. 'We've kept it quiet so that my mother wouldn't find out. She hates the Taylors. And she hates the fact that we're having to struggle to pay for my gran's nursing home fees, while they've got the Abbey. You'd think the Taylors stole it from us, the way my mother talks, but they're just business people who saw that it was up for sale and bought it. The thing is, the wages I get from my job aren't enough to cover the fees, so David has been giving me money. My mother thought all along that it was money I earned, but a lot of it was coming from David. He wanted to

122

help me. Except that I found out last week that he had borrowed the money he was giving me.'

'Borrowed it from where?' asked Holly.

'From a loan shark,' said Samantha. 'I was so angry when he told me. We had a terrible row. The really awful thing is that the man wants the money back. He wants it back straightaway, but David hasn't got it. David and I nearly split up over it. I thought we were never going to see each other again. But I wanted to try and help him. He would never have borrowed the money in the first place if he hadn't been trying to help me. It was all my fault.'

'Harry Owen,' breathed Holly. 'He borrowed the money from Harry Owen.'

Samantha shook her head. 'I don't know the name,' she said. 'All I know is that David is in trouble. That's why I took your copy of the painting. I was going to give it to David. I thought that we might have been able to work out the clues between us. I thought that if we could find the painting of the White Lady, David might be able to sell it and pay off his debts. But when I phoned David that evening, he wouldn't talk to me. He was still angry with me because I'd called him a fool for having borrowed the money. So I gave the copy back to you, and told you about the brooch, in the hope that you'd pass the story on to him.'

'But the painting belongs to the school,' said Holly. 'Even if you had found it, it wouldn't have helped David.'

'I know,' said Samantha. 'But I had to try and do something. In the end I couldn't just leave things the way they were between us. When I saw him outside the school the other afternoon with you and the others, I was sure he wanted to see me again. That's why I went up to the Abbey yesterday evening. David is trying to be cool about it, but I can tell he's frightened. He's had threats, Holly. They've threatened to hurt him if he doesn't pay up. I'm really scared for him.'

'He should go to the police,' said Holly.

'That's what I told him,' said Samantha. 'But he's afraid that they'll get to him before the police can act. He told me he's going to try and reason with them one more time.' Samantha swallowed hard, her voice shaking. 'He said he's going to meet with the man this evening.' She reached out and caught hold of Holly's wrist. 'You promise you won't tell anyone about this?'

'I wish there was something we could do,' said Holly. 'But unless he's prepared to go to the police –'

'Well, if it isn't our star journalist.' It was Steffie Smith's voice. 'Cooking up some new item for *Winformation*, are you?'

Holly looked round at Steffie. She had come up behind them as silent as a cat.

'Found that old painting yet?' said Steffie mockingly.

'No. Not yet,' said Holly. 'But don't worry. When I do, I'll be writing about it for you.'

'I shouldn't bother,' said Steffie. 'Your last piece wasn't up to much. I don't know if I'll bother to print anything else by you. Not unless you learn to write properly.'

Holly glared at her. 'If my writing was as bad as yours, I think I'd be the last person to go around criticising anyone,' she said, standing up. 'And if you don't mind, I've got better things to do than stand here arguing with you.'

She walked out of the library, not giving Steffie a chance to reply.

The Mystery Club met in Holly's bedroom that evening. The main topic of conversation had changed from their search for the stolen painting to David Taylor's problems with Harry Owen.

'If that man's going around threatening people,' said Tracy, 'we ought to do something about it. There are laws about things like that.'

'Do you mean we should tell the police?' said Belinda.

'We should at least try and convince David to go to them,' said Holly. 'Samantha said he's going to try and reason with Owen one more time. But if what I heard in the churchyard is right, it's not Owen that's after David – it's that man Barney.'

'Do you think David knows that?' said Tracy.

'Of course he does,' said Holly. 'That's why he was so defensive the other night at the Abbey. He knew perfectly well who the trespasser was. I suspected it all along. That was how he knew about the eagle on the leather jacket.'

Belinda put her hand over her mouth. 'We probably saved him from being beaten up,' she said.

'We've got to do something,' said Tracy angrily. 'I wish there was some way of helping David.' She suddenly stopped her pacing up and down the room. 'Listen, you guys, David's going to see Harry Owen this evening, right? Well, why don't we catch him before he gets there? We could try and convince him to go to the police.' She looked at her two friends. 'What do you say?'

Belinda looked at Holly. 'She might have an idea, you know.'

'We've got to be quick,' said Tracy. 'We've got to leave like now if we're going to get to Owen's place before David does.'

'Let's get over there, then,' said Holly, grabbing her coat. 'This is our chance for some real detective work.'

'I hope we're not too late,' said Holly. They were standing in the main street, near the side road where she had seen David with Harry Owen.

The weather had improved from the storms over the weekend, but there was still a lot of cloud about, and it was chilly in the narrow streets as the evening came on.

'Keep your fingers crossed,' said Tracy, looking up and down the street.

'I'm keeping everything crossed,' said Belinda. She looked at her watch. They had been standing on the street corner for half an hour. There had been no sign of David's rickety old convertible.

'You don't suppose he's been and gone, do you?' said Holly.

'I doubt it,' said Tracy. 'The Abbey doesn't close until half past five. Even if he left straightaway he wouldn't have got here much before six.' She looked at her watch. 'It's only half past now. Just be patient, you guys. He'll be here, don't worry.'

Holly pushed her hands into her jacket pockets and edged to the corner to have another quick look down the side road. There was a blue car parked opposite the narrow doorway where she had seen Owen with David the other day. They hadn't paid any attention to it. They were waiting for David's car.

As Holly glanced over her shoulder she saw David getting into the blue car.

'What?' she cried, grabbing at her friends. 'Look!'

As she pulled them to the corner, the strange car revved its engine and sped away from them.

'That's not David's car,' exclaimed Tracy. 'What's that dumb idiot doing coming here in the wrong car?'

'We've missed him,' said Belinda. 'He was in there all the time, and we've been standing out here like three lemons.'

'Worse than that,' said Holly. 'I saw that car go

127

down there, but I never thought to look who was driving it. Some brilliant detectives we are.'

They looked at one another in confusion. 'Now what?' said Belinda.

'I'm going down there,' said Tracy. 'I want a closer look at that place.'

'Don't be crazy,' said Holly. 'Owen might see you.'

'So what?' said Tracy. 'He doesn't know me. You're the only one he's seen. I want to see if there's a sign or something on that door that might give us some idea of who this Owen guy is.'

'Tracy!' hissed Holly. 'Don't be mad!'

But it was too late. Tracy was already striding down the side road towards the narrow black door.

'We can't let her go on her own,' said Belinda, following Tracy. With a worried frown, Holly went after her two friends.

Tracy was at the door. She bent over and pushed the letter-box open.

Just then the door opened and Tracy nearly fell into the dark hallway.

Holly grabbed Belinda and pulled her out of sight into the safety of a sunken doorway only a few feet away from the open door.

'What do you want?' Holly recognised the harsh, grating voice of Harry Owen. She pressed herself against the wall and hoped he wouldn't look in their direction.

'Hi, there,' she heard Tracy say. 'I'm doing a project for my school. I wonder if I could ask you a few questions about your opinion of the education system in this area?'

'She's got some nerve,' whispered Belinda.

'Shh!' hissed Holly. 'It's him.'

'Holly Adams!' said a familiar, high-pitched voice. Holly jumped. It was Steffie Smith. She was standing at the corner of the main street, staring down the side road at Holly and Belinda. 'I want a word with you!' she said.

Steffie came marching across the road. 'What are you skulking about in there for, anyway? Hot on the trail of that stupid painting, are you?'

Holly gave her her fiercest look. 'Go away!' she whispered.

'Don't tell me to go away,' declared Steffie. 'We've got some business to sort out about what you said yesterday morning. I know you've been avoiding me. Scared, are you?'

Holly glanced over her shoulder. Tracy was standing there with her mouth half open. Harry Owen was staring at Holly, frowning heavily.

A look of recognition crossed his face. He pushed past Tracy and walked ponderously towards Holly, his mouth set in a hard line.

'What's the game? You were here with the Taylor boy, weren't you?' he growled. He looked back at Tracy, then at the others, his eyes finally settling coldly on Holly.

'Are you looking for trouble?' he said grimly. 'Because if you are, you've come to the right place.'

13 Steffie saves the day

'Just a minute,' Steffie said angrily, staring up at the bull-necked man with her hands firmly on her hips. 'I was here first, if you don't mind!'

A ripple of surprise crossed his face. He was obviously not used to being spoken to like that.

'Keep your mouth shut,' he said. 'Unless you want trouble as well.' His eyes fixed on Holly. 'I've seen you around too often. What's your game?' His mouth spread in a humourless grin. 'Has that Taylor boy got you spying on me? Is that what it is?'

Tracy ran up to him. 'David doesn't even know we're here,' she said.

'Tracy!' said Belinda.

Owen nodded. 'So it's *David*, is it?' He laughed. It wasn't a pleasant sound. He scratched his cheek and stared hard at Holly. 'Your friend David has been a very silly boy. I don't like being spied on. You tell him – '

'Excuse me!' Steffie interrupted. 'I don't like your attitude, mister. If you don't go away I'll call my father. He's only over there.' She pointed across the main road. 'And, for your information, my father is the Chief Constable of the entire county. I'm sure he'd be more than happy to talk to you about your threatening behaviour.'

Harry Owen gave her a deadly look. Steffie didn't even blink.

He switched his gaze to Holly. 'You can tell Taylor from me that this little episode has made me change my mind. Just tell him that. I've changed my mind.'

'I don't know what you mean,' said Holly.

'Don't you?' said Owen. He shook his head. 'It doesn't matter whether you know what I mean or not. Just tell the Taylor boy what I said.' He turned, pushing past Tracy and walking back to the open door.

'You tell him that!' he shouted. The door slammed behind him.

'What a creep,' said Steffie.

'Your dad's not a policeman,' said Belinda to Steffie. 'He works in a butcher's shop.'

'True,' said Steffie. 'But melon-head didn't know that.' She looked at Holly. 'I think we'll finish our conversation in private some other time.' One eyebrow lifted. 'I can't say I'm impressed by your choice of friends.'

'He's not my friend,' said Holly. 'But thanks for getting rid of him.'

Steffie snorted. 'That wasn't for your benefit,' she said. 'I can't stand people who interrupt me.' She turned on her heel. 'I haven't finished with you, Holly Adams,' she said. 'Our little chat is only postponed.'

They watched as she strode away out of sight.

'Well,' said Belinda. 'What a turn up. Saved by Steffie Smith. You'll have to put that in the magazine, Holly.'

'It's not funny,' said Holly. 'We could have got ourselves into real trouble.' She looked at Tracy. 'Fancy peering through his letter-box.'

'I didn't know he was going to jump out at me,' said Tracy.

'And then admitting we know David,' said Belinda. 'We might have got away with it otherwise.'

'You've got to be kidding me!' said Tracy. 'He had us buttoned down from the moment Steffie Smith got involved and he caught sight of Holly. But what do you think he meant that he's changed his mind?'

'So much for helping David,' said Holly. 'We've made it worse now. David had probably made some deal with that man, and now we've come along and ruined it. If something bad happens to him, it's going to be our fault.'

It was clear to Holly and the others that David had to be warned about what had happened. And warned very quickly. Phone calls to the Abbey that evening received no response. In the end Holly suggested that their best bet would be to tell Samantha what had happened and get her to contact David.

The next morning at school they searched for Samantha. She was in none of her usual haunts.

Holly went to her form teacher. She came back to Tracy and Belinda with bad news.

'Samantha's mother phoned in,' she told them. 'Samantha's off school. Apparently her gran's had a bad turn.'

'Now what do we do?' said Belinda.

'I think we should go up there,' said Holly. 'Go up to the Abbey after school.'

'I can't this afternoon,' said Tracy. 'I've promised to help my mom in the nursery.'

'I've got to go home too,' said Belinda. 'My dad's off on one of his business trips abroad, and my mother will go crazy if I'm not there to say goodbye to him.'

'I'll go on my own,' said Holly. 'I'll get Jamie to tell my dad I'll be a bit late home.'

It seemed like a very long day to Holly as she waited for school to end. She saw her friends briefly as she finally headed for the bus stop.

'You'll be careful, won't you?' said Tracy.

'Of course,' said Holly. 'And if I can't find him, I'll leave a note.'

Holly sat staring out of the window as the bus crawled its way out of town. She wasn't looking forward to her encounter with David. She hadn't spoken to him since their argument the other evening, and now she was going to have to tell him that their escapade at Harry Owen's office had ruined whatever deal he had made with the man. It wasn't going to be a very comfortable interview.

Holly asked for David at the paydesk.

'He's over in the old barn,' she was told. 'Playing with that balloon again. He's been there all day.'

The barn was part of a collection of old buildings in a hollow on the far side of the Abbey. Holly found David there with a couple of other men, hauling heavy gas canisters about.

'Hello,' said Holly. 'Can we talk?'

David straightened up. He led Holly outside. 'I'm glad you came,' he said. 'I wanted to apologise for what I said the other night.'

Holly smiled bleakly. 'You might change your mind about that when you hear what I've got to tell you.'

They sat on some logs outside the barn. Holly told him everything that had happened. About the conversation she had heard between Harry Owen and the man called Barney. About Samantha telling her of the money he had borrowed, and lastly about the disastrous meeting with Harry Owen the previous evening.

David sat with his head in his hands.

'I'm sorry,' said Holly. 'We were only trying to help. We wanted to speak to you before you met with Owen. We were watching for your car all the time.'

'I borrowed Robert's car,' said David softly, drawing his hands over his face. 'Come with me. I want to show you something.'

He took her over to another building. He hauled the doors open. There was his old car.

He pointed to the wheels. All four tyres had been slashed. 'That was another warning to pay up,' he said. 'That was what made me decide to go and see Owen.' He laughed hollowly. 'I made a deal with him. He was going to lend me enough money to pay that other man off.' A bleak expression passed over his face. 'At two hundred per cent interest. I would probably have been years paying it off, but at least it would have got that lunatic off my back. But it sounds like Owen's not going to help me now.' He gave Holly a bitter look. 'I told you to mind your own business, didn't I?'

'You should go to the police,' said Holly.

'Yes,' said David. 'And I could give my evidence from a hospital bed.' He slammed his fist down on the bonnet of the car. 'I was only trying to help Samantha,' he said. He leaned heavily over the car. 'Oh, it's not your fault,' he said, looking sideways at her. 'I'm not blaming you. Owen's a crook. I was stupid. I was so eager to get my hands on that money that I didn't even realise how much I'd have to pay back. I could even have coped with it if this other man hadn't come along wanting the whole lot in one go.'

'What are you going to do?' asked Holly.

'I could leave town,' said David. 'Run away.' He turned and leaned against the car, staring out of the double doors up at the Abbey. 'Don't worry about me. I got myself into this. I'll get myself out.'

'Why won't you go to the police?' asked Holly. 'Surely that's the best bet.'

'You don't know what that Barney is capable of,' said David. 'You've seen what he's done to my car. And, come on, you're not stupid. How do you think that rat got in there? That was one of Barney's calling cards. And the next thing he'll do is put me in hospital. I've got to get out of here. I can stall him for a few days, I think. That'll give me time to arrange something.' He saw the worried look on Holly's face. 'It's OK,' he said. 'Barney won't get me.'

David walked out of the building. 'And meanwhile,' he said. 'Robert and I have still got to put on a demonstration with the Red Devil tomorrow afternoon.'

'I don't know how you can think of something like that the way things are,' said Holly, following him into the open.

'We've got coach parties coming,' said David. 'We can't disappoint the punters.' He smiled round at her. 'I'll understand if you don't want to, but I'd like it if you and your friends could come over

136

tomorrow. You could have that ride I promised you. And you can tell me how you're getting on in your search for the *White Lady*.'

'That doesn't seem very important now,' said Holly.

'I don't know about that,' said David. 'If I were to find it, I could sneak off and sell it and pay my debts with the proceeds. Just like old Roderick was intending to do all those years ago.'

'That was Samantha's idea as well, but the painting belongs to the school,' Holly reminded him.

'I know,' said David. 'I was only joking. Listen, while you're here, could you do me a favour?'

'I don't know what I can do to help,' said Holly.

'It's nothing to do with what we've been talking about,' said David. 'Come up to the house with me. I don't want to go into town – I don't want to accidentally meet that Barney before I have to. But I promised to give some things to the library.'

They walked up to the Abbey.

'Did you know they're having an exhibition of old photographs in town?' said David.

'Yes,' said Holly. 'My dad mentioned it.'

'I've agreed to let them have some of our old photo albums. It's stuff that no one's looked at for years. There's bound to be some interesting pictures in amongst it all. If I give them to you, will you take them down there for me?'

'Yes, of course,' said Holly, following David up to the private part of the house.

Holly leafed through the crackly pages of brownish photographs.

There were scenes of Willow Dale as it had looked many years ago. There were stiff, formal portraits of solemn-faced people staring fixedly into the camera.

'Who are these?' asked Holly. She had turned over a page to a sepia-tinted photograph of a row of stern-faced young women in black gowns.

'I've no idea,' said David. 'Like I told you, no one has looked at these albums for years.'

'It's a pity there aren't explanations with the photos,' said Holly. She looked more closely at the line of staring women.

'David,' she breathed softly. 'Look.' She pointed to one of the women. 'I know that face.'

David leaned over her shoulder. 'Perhaps you've seen her in a horror movie – she's the stoniest-faced one of the lot. She looks as if her jaw would fall off if she smiled.'

'It's almost exactly like the face of the White Lady,' said Holly. She looked round at David. 'She's older than in the painting, but I'd swear it was her.'

'Hold on a minute,' said David. Very carefully he slid the aged photograph out of its black paper frame. He turned it over.

On the back, in ink that had faded to an almost

invisible brown, was written, 'The headmistress and staff of the Winifred Bowen-Davies School for Young Women.'

They looked at each other.

'You realise what this means?' said David. 'If you're right, it means that the White Lady was a teacher at your school.'

'That would make sense,' breathed Holly. 'If she was the governess to Hugo Bastable's children, then she might well have gone off to become a schoolteacher.'

The telephone rang. David went to answer it while Holly looked again at the solemn face of the unknown teacher.

'Yes,' she heard David say, 'I understand.' He put the receiver down.

Holly looked round at him. His face was ashen white.

'What was it?' asked Holly.

'I've got to go somewhere,' he said, his voice shaking.

'Was it *him*?' asked Holly.

'He wants to meet me,' said David.

'You should go to the police,' said Holly.

David nodded. 'I will,' he said. 'I'll give you a lift back into town and go straight to the police station.'

Holly took the photograph albums and they went to the car that David had borrowed. They drove into town in silence.

'Good luck,' said Holly as she climbed out.

David nodded, but didn't speak. She watched as the car drove along the road.

She frowned. She didn't know Willow Dale all that well, but she did know that the police station was in the centre of the town.

So why was it that David was driving back towards the outskirts? If he wasn't going to the police, where was he going?

14 *The Red Devil*

'I'm sure David didn't go to the police,' said Holly.
It was the following morning. Holly had waited for
her friends outside the school and had told them
everything that had passed between her and David
the previous evening, including the telephone call
from the man called Barney.

'There's nothing we can do now,' said Tracy.
'Either he'll go to the police or he won't.'

'She's right,' said Belinda. 'We've done everything we can.'

'I know,' said Holly. 'And I suppose we'll find
out what's happened soon enough, but I can't help
thinking some of it is our fault.'

'We didn't get him to borrow the money in the
first place,' said Belinda.

'Do you really think he'll do a runner?' said
Tracy. 'That's not the answer, surely?'

'I don't know,' said Holly. 'I don't know what
he might do.'

The only bright spot in all of this was the latest
clue that Holly had found to the identity of the
White Lady.

141

'But it seems so futile,' she told her friends. 'Hunting around for a missing painting while all this trouble is going on.'

'Well,' said Belinda. 'We can't do anything for David. But we can carry on looking for the *White Lady*.' She shrugged. 'At least it'll take our minds off it.'

'So what should we do?' asked Tracy.

'I think we should see Miss Horswell,' said Holly.

'I must say,' said Miss Horswell, 'I'm very impressed by the commitment you girls are showing in your hunt for our lost painting.'

Holly, Tracy and Belinda were in the head-teacher's office. They had just told her of Holly's latest discovery.

'And of course,' Miss Horswell continued, 'we have records of the names of everyone who taught here. But whether you'll be able to trace them after all this time is another matter entirely. They'll all be long dead. If the photograph you saw is as old as you say I doubt whether any information we could give you would be of use.'

'But we can go through the records, can we?' asked Holly.

'With pleasure,' said Miss Horswell.

'You realise this means another trip down to that grotty basement,' said Belinda as they left Miss Horswell's office. 'My mother will have a fit if I go home looking like I've been down a coal mine again. She still hasn't forgiven me for ruining that coat.'

'Like you said,' pointed out Tracy, 'it'll take our minds off David.' She looked at her friends. 'Are we going up to the Abbey this afternoon?'

'I think we should,' said Holly. 'At least to check out whether he's all right.'

'And to have a ride in the Red Devil, if that's still on,' said Tracy.

'How you can think about messing about in that balloon when all this is going on beats me,' said Belinda.

'David's got to take it up today anyway,' said Holly. 'They've got coach parties going up to the Abbey especially. They'll all be demanding their money back if it's a nice day and he doesn't give them a display.'

'I'm not missing my chance for a ride in the Red Devil,' said Tracy. 'And that Barney guy won't be able to get at him up in the air, will he? And there'll be loads of other people around. He'll probably be safer up in the Red Devil than he would anywhere else right now.'

They found lists of scores of teachers in the thick black books that lined the basement shelves. Holly scribbled the names down in the Mystery Club's notebook. Names that went right back into the last century. Whittling the lists down was going to be a long process.

'The next step is to go to the town hall,' said Holly. 'They must have records that will help us trace them. We might be able discover where the White Lady lived,' said Holly. 'You never know – Roderick might have stashed the stolen painting with her. If we had her address we could go there and look.'

'But if she was young in old Hugo's time, she'd probably have been dead by the time Roderick was around,' said Belinda. 'Don't you think you're being a bit over-optimistic?'

'Got any better ideas?' asked Holly. 'I'm just trying to follow the clues.'

'None that spring to mind,' said Belinda. 'But we haven't got all the clues. We still don't know what that design on the folly is all about.'

'I bet you anything you like it'll be the plan of the White Lady's house,' said Holly. 'Just you wait.'

A fresh breeze ruffled the treetops as they made their way down to the high iron gates of the Abbey.

'They've got some crowds in,' said Belinda. The car park was full and there were streams of people making their way up the hill to the house.

The three girls could soon see the Red Devil as they mounted the long slope. The roar of the flames was carried to them by the breeze.

'I hope it won't be too windy,' said Tracy.

The balloon was tethered by a dozen or more

sturdy ropes. It rocked gently, its silky sides billowing as the hot air rose up into its hollow heart. Crowds of people were gathered around.

David was hammering a final peg into the grass. He smiled when he saw them. 'Great,' he said. 'I'm glad you came.'

'What happened about the police?' asked Holly.

David frowned at her. 'I'll tell you later,' he said.

'You didn't *go* to the police, did you?' said Holly.

'Can we talk about this some other time?' said David. 'I'm OK, aren't I? You can see nothing's happened to me.'

Holly looked suspiciously at him, but there were too many people around for her to try and get any more out of him at the moment.

'Is the weather all right for ballooning?' asked Tracy, looking up at the immense red globe as it strained at its guy ropes.

'The forecast is for clear skies,' said David. 'There's a bit of a wind, but it shouldn't be a problem. Another ten minutes and we'll be off. Come with me and I'll get you fitted with helmets.'

'Not for me,' said Belinda. 'I'm only watching.'

'Don't be such a coward,' said Tracy. 'I wouldn't miss this for the world.'

'It's perfectly safe,' said David.

'Then why do we need helmets?' asked Belinda.

145

'I can't imagine they'll do much good if you fall out at a few hundred feet.'

'No one has ever fallen out,' said David.

'There's always a first time,' muttered Belinda.

They followed David under the huge canopy. The roar of the flames made conversation almost impossible.

Suddenly the noise stopped. David spoke to a man in the balloon. He beckoned the three girls over.

'We're ready,' he said. 'All aboard.'

Tracy clambered into the basket. 'Right,' she said. 'Grab her, Holly!'

'No! Wait! Hang on!' yelled Belinda as Holly caught her from behind and Tracy leaned out of the basket to catch hold of her arms.

'You're coming with us,' said Holly, giving Belinda a shove that sent her over the edge of the basket.

Belinda clung on to the edge, struggling to pull herself out. 'Get off me, you maniacs!' she shouted, fighting to get her arms free from Tracy's grip.

'You'd never forgive yourself if you missed out on a chance like this,' laughed Tracy, pulling her on board. 'You'll thank us for this afterwards.'

'I won't,' wailed Belinda. 'I'll kill you.' She made a last attempt to escape, but now both Tracy and Holly had a firm hold on her.

David climbed aboard.

'Ropes away!' he shouted. All around the balloon men began to disengage the guy ropes.

'It's a conspiracy!' yelled Belinda. 'I'm being kidnapped.'

'Be quiet,' said Tracy, 'and put this helmet on.'

'Holly Adams, I'm never going to forgive you for this,' said Belinda. 'I knew Tracy was as mad as a hatter, but I thought you – oh! Help!' The basket shifted and Belinda clutched at Holly.

David laughed. 'Too late to get off now,' he shouted as the air rocked with a blast of flame from the gas jets.

'You had this planned, didn't you?' said Belinda. 'All of you. All along.'

'I'm afraid so,' said Holly.

Belinda covered her eyes with both hands. 'I'll be sick,' she warned. 'I get vertigo standing on a ten pence piece. I can't look.'

The balloon rose majestically into the air to the cheering of the crowds. Tracy hung over the side, waving to the upturned faces as they slid away. 'This is fabulous!' she said.

'Don't lean over too far,' said David. 'We don't want to lose you. Well, Robert?' he asked the other man. 'Is everything OK?'

'Perfect,' said Robert, grinning at Belinda. She was trying to keep her eyes covered whilst steadying herself with one white-knuckled hand holding the edge of the basket.

'There,' said Tracy, poking Belinda in the ribs. 'What did we tell you? Is this fun or what?'

'I'm not looking,' said Belinda. 'Just tell me when it's all over.'

The grounds of the Abbey fell away beneath them, spread out like a table-top model. The crowds of people seemed no bigger than thimbles. Roads ran like ribbon through patchwork green fields, curling to and fro as they climbed the rugged hills that capped the peaceful valley.

Holly gazed down, watching the Abbey and the other buildings around it shrink into toys. Away in the distance she could see the town of Willow Dale.

Robert turned off the gas jets and suddenly everything was silent.

'What's happened?' moaned Belinda. 'Are we going to crash?'

'Open your eyes and you'll find out,' said David.

'It's wonderful,' said Holly, shielding her eyes against the sunlight. 'I can see the ice rink. Look!'

The breeze was taking them towards the town. 'Belinda, you're missing it all. Look – that's the cinema. You can see absolutely everything from up here.'

Belinda uncovered one eye.

'Can you see my house?' said Tracy. She pointed down. 'It should be around there somewhere. Belinda, look! There's the church.'

148

The balloon rose higher and made its way slowly across the town, its shadow rippling over the buildings as it sailed along.

Belinda uncovered her other eye and dared a quick glance down. 'Look!' she said. 'There's a bus. Wow! This *is* amazing. And look over there – it's the school. Let's give Miss Horswell a wave.'

'I thought you were supposed to be scared of heights,' said Tracy.

'I thought I was,' said Belinda, leaning over to watch the streets and houses of the town sliding by beneath them.

Belinda's hand grabbed at Holly's sleeve. 'Holly!' she shouted.

'Don't do that,' said Holly. 'You're not going to fall out.'

'I know. But look. Look at the school! Can't you see it?'

The three girls looked down as the school slid away under the basket.

'What?' asked Holly. 'What am I supposed to be looking at?'

'Look at the shape of the grounds around the school,' cried Belinda. 'It's the same shape as on the folly! It's exactly the same pattern as on the painting. That design was a map of the school!'

15   Mr Barnard's confession

'It is!' yelled Belinda, clutching at her friends. 'You see? The outer wall, the school building itself, the tennis courts, the paths – they're all exactly like the squares and lines on the folly! We've solved the final clue!'

'But how would Roderick have known what the school looked like from the air?' said Tracy.

'He wouldn't,' said Belinda. 'He would have done exactly what I did. He'd have found out from a map. Remember when I first saw the design I said it looked like a map of somewhere? I checked that it wasn't the Abbey, but I never thought to look at any other buildings. Roderick must have copied the design from a map of the school.'

'The school,' breathed Holly. 'Of course. It all fits. The painting is hidden somewhere at the school. Old Roderick must have taken it out of its frame and hidden it somewhere in the school grounds, meaning to come back for it later.'

'It makes sense,' said Tracy. 'He must have known he'd be suspect number one, and that the police would be swarming all over him as soon as the painting went missing. He must have intended to pick it up when all the fuss had died down.'

'But the police caught up with him for fraud before he could retrieve it,' said David. 'And it's been sitting there ever since. So all those people who hunted in the Abbey were *miles* out.'

The three girls moved round the basket, watching the school as the balloon passed above it.

Belinda turned to look at David. 'I realise this is probably a very silly question,' she said. 'But how do we get this thing back to the Abbey?'

David smiled. 'We don't,' he said. 'We can only go where the wind blows us.'

Belinda gave him an anxious look.

'Don't fret,' said David. 'Robert knows what he's doing. Don't you, Robert?'

'I hope so,' said Robert with a grin. 'You probably won't be able to spot it now, because we're going over the town, but there's a truck shadowing us. When we come down, we'll be picked up in the truck and taken back.'

'I hope we don't end up perched in the top of a tree,' said Belinda.

'I don't think we will,' said Robert. 'I've worked out the wind speed and direction, so unless something unexpected happens, we'll be landing on Brooke's Field.'

'I know it,' said Belinda. 'But it's about ten miles away.'

'So we won't be back for ages,' said Holly. She

shrugged. 'Oh, well,' she said. 'I suppose we might as well enjoy the view then. Unless we fancy jumping out.'

The balloon drifted slowly away from Willow Dale and out over open countryside. Occasionally Robert would give a blast of hot air to maintain their height.

'I see the truck,' said Tracy. A large vehicle was moving along an otherwise almost empty thread of road.

'Yes,' said David. 'That's it. I'm afraid it'll take us a while to collapse the Red Devil and pack it all away.'

Robert began to release air from the balloon, pulling on a rope that opened a vent in the top and let the heated air out.

Very gradually they sank towards the ground.

'That's where we're landing,' said Robert, pointing to a wide level area of tall grass. 'It'll be a bit bumpy. I should hang on to something.'

'I can't look,' said Belinda.

The ground was suddenly much closer, the grass streaming away beneath them.

'Hang on!' called David.

There was a rush and a thud and a series of jolting bounces. The balloon's tall sides wavered and blew as Robert let the air pour out.

They were safely down.

Holly and her friends helped David and Robert until they heard the truck drive up. Four young men jumped out, and between them, everyone got on with the heavy work of folding the deflated balloon and loading it into the back.

All nine of them crammed into the truck. Holly, Belinda, Tracy and two of the men sat in the back, cushioned on the thick folded material of the balloon.

David shouted to them through a small window in the back of the truck's cab. 'OK if we drop you just outside the Abbey?' he asked. 'You'll be able to get a bus from there, won't you?'

'Yes,' said Holly. 'That'll be fine.'

The three girls talked excitedly of how and where they should search.

'Roderick can't have had time to hide it anywhere terribly complicated,' said Belinda. 'I mean, it's not going to be bricked up behind a wall, or under the floorboards or anything.'

'It'll be in a basement room, I bet,' said Tracy. 'Like the one where we found the copy. Some disused old room that no one's been in for years.'

'Or perhaps he could have slid it under a carpet,' suggested Holly. 'Or hidden it up in the attics.'

The truck came to a halt and the back doors were flung open.

The girls scrambled out.

They had stopped on the main road, near the gravel pathway that led down to the gates of the Abbey. On the other side a grey car was parked.

A man got out of the car and walked slowly over to them.

The three girls stared at him in amazement. It was Mr Barnard's brother, Tom. His hands were thrust into the pockets of a leather jacket.

'What's he doing here?' said Tracy. 'Ow! Holly, you're hurting me.' Holly's fingers were gripping Tracy's arm.

'The jacket,' whispered Holly.

Tom Barnard walked past them as if they didn't exist and stood facing David. The girls could clearly see the design of the eagle on the back of the jacket, its wings spread and its head lowered in flight.

'Been for a ride, have you?' said Tom Barnard. 'I thought we had an appointment.'

'I said I'd meet you tomorrow,' replied David, his voice shaking.

'I got impatient,' said Tom Barnard.

Robert stood beside David. 'Is there a problem?' he asked.

'No,' said David quietly. 'No problem.'

Tom Barnard gave Robert a casual glance. 'That's right,' he said. 'We're not going to have any problems here, are we?'

The other four men lined up behind David. Tom Barnard looked slowly from face to face.

'I'm doing a bit of business with Mr Taylor,' he said with a cold smile. 'I don't think we'll be needing your help.'

Robert looked at David. 'Is there anything we can do?'

David shook his head. 'No. It's OK.' He lifted his head and looked into Tom Barnard's closed face. 'I said tomorrow,' he said. 'Come back tomorrow and we'll sort everything out. Don't worry, everything will be ready for you.'

The icy smile came and went on Tom Barnard's face. 'I'm not worried,' he said. 'I never worry. I let other people do my worrying for me. Know what I mean?'

'I know what you mean,' said David, his face white.

'Good,' said Tom Barnard. 'Then we understand each other.'

He turned and walked back to the car. Holly let out a long breath. As he opened the car door, Tom Barnard turned and spoke again.

'I'll be back,' he said. He climbed into the car and drove off.

'What was all that about?' asked Robert.

'Nothing I can't handle,' said David. 'You take the van down to the Abbey. I'll be along in a minute. I just want to have a word with the girls.'

Holly waited until the van was bumping its way down the gravel pathway. 'Barney!' she said. 'It was Mr Barnard's brother all along.'

'Mr Barnard's brother,' breathed Tracy. 'I can't believe it. Do you think he knows? Do you think Mr Barnard knows what his brother is up to?'

'You know him?' said David.

'His brother is a teacher at our school,' said Belinda.

'You were going to the police,' said Holly. 'You said you were going to the police.'

David lifted his hands. 'I'm sorry,' he said. 'I did mean to go to the police, but in the end I was too scared. I met with Barney. I pretended I could get him the money. It's OK. I'm leaving Willow Dale first thing in the morning. He won't find me.'

'So you're going to run?' said Holly. 'You're going to let him and Owen get away with it?'

'I'm not a hero, Holly,' said David. 'I know I should go to the police, but I'm scared of what will happen to me if I inform on these men. All I need to do is get away from here and everything will be all right.'

'That's just cowardly,' said Tracy.

'Yes,' said David bitterly. 'It's cowardly. I don't expect you to understand. I'm scared. I'm scared of what that man will do. If that makes me a coward, then fine. I'm a coward.' He looked at the three friends, his face pale and unhappy. 'At least *try* to understand,' he said. 'What else can I do?'

'You know what you should do,' said Holly. She looked at Tracy and Belinda. 'I'm going home,' she said.

David watched as they walked away from him.

'Are we really going to do nothing?' asked Belinda. 'Surely we could do something?'

'You heard him,' said Tracy. 'What can we do?'

'We could go and speak to Mr Barnard,' said Holly. 'Maybe David isn't prepared to go to the police, but I can't believe that Mr Barnard would keep something like this quiet.'

'But what if he already knows all about it?' said Belinda.

Holly shook her head. 'I don't believe that,' she said. 'I'm going to Mr Barnard's house, and I'm going to tell him about his brother.'

'Oh, Holly,' said Tracy. 'I hope this is a good idea. What if his brother went straight home? He might be there.'

'If we see the car we'll leave it until the morning,' said Holly.

They were very subdued on the bus back into town. As they walked along the leafy avenue towards Mr Barnard's bungalow, birds were singing their evening songs. The low sun stretched peaceful shadows in their path, but it was impossible for the three girls to feel calm as they made their way down the road.

'The car isn't there,' said Belinda. 'He can't have got back yet.' She shivered. 'I don't like this,' she said. 'What if he turns up while we're still here?'

'He'd be crazy to touch us,' said Tracy.

Holly took a deep breath and lifted the knocker. 'Let's hope he isn't crazy,' she said.

The door opened.

Mr Barnard stared at them in astonishment.

'We need to talk to you,' said Holly, sounding a lot cooler than she felt. 'It's about your brother.'

'My brother?' said Mr Barnard. 'What on earth . . .?'

'He's a crook,' blurted Tracy.

There was a moment of dreadful silence. 'Get in here,' Mr Barnard said finally. They filed into his hallway. He closed the door and stood with his back to it, his piercing eyes raking over them. 'What on earth do you think you're doing, coming here like this?' he demanded.

'It's true,' said Tracy. 'Tell him, Holly.'

'I heard your brother talking to a man called Harry Owen,' Holly began hesitantly. Mr Barnard's expression changed from anger to deep unease as she told him her story.

'It's all true,' said Belinda. 'Every word of it. David is really frightened of him.'

Mr Barnard's hand came up and touched his injured eye. 'I see,' he said in a low voice. 'And who else have you told about this?'

'No one,' said Holly. 'We told David to go to the police, but he's too scared of what your brother might do to him. We thought you would help.'

Mr Barnard leaned back against the door, his eyes staring out over their heads.

'You knew about this, didn't you?' said Tracy. 'You knew all about it.'

'No,' said Mr Barnard. 'Not everything.' He gazed at them, desperation in his eyes. 'I wish you hadn't found out about this,' he said. 'I hoped Tom would get what he came for and leave without anyone knowing. He's only just got out of prison, you see. He told me he needed somewhere to stay while he finished off some business with a man he used to have dealings with. I knew it was something bad, but I didn't think it would involve other people. I even tried to get rid of him myself. I told him to go.' He gestured to his bruised face. 'I wasn't mugged,' he said. 'Tom did this.'

The three girls gasped.

'I didn't want to be involved,' Mr Barnard continued. 'I was thinking of my reputation. I didn't want it coming out that my brother was a criminal.' Mr Barnard shook his head. 'I didn't realise what he was up to.' He looked at them with sudden determination in his face. 'This must stop,' he said. 'I can't carry on covering up for him. It's gone too far. You had better get off home, girls. I'm going to call the police.'

He opened the front door. The three girls went out on to the path.

'Don't worry,' said Mr Barnard. 'I'll sort it out. But please do one thing for me. Don't tell anyone else about this. Let me deal with it. It will be much safer for you if Tom never knows you were involved.'

The three friends walked to the end of the street.

'Did he look sick or what?' said Tracy.

'Do you blame him?' said Belinda. 'I'd feel pretty sick myself if I had a brother like that.'

'And I thought *my* brother was a pain,' said Holly.

Her two friends looked at her and smiled bleakly.

Without warning, Holly suddenly gasped and grabbed at her friends, pulling them under the cover of some bushes. They followed the line of her eyes.

Tom Barnard's car drove down the avenue.

'Do you think he saw us?' said Tracy.

'I hope not,' said Holly. 'I really hope not.' She leaned out of cover and saw the car stop outside Mr Barnard's house. The car door opened and she watched as Tom Barnard walked up the path.

'I wouldn't want to be Mr Barnard right now,' said Tracy.

'Let's get out of here,' said Belinda.

'No,' said Holly. 'Wait a minute.'

'What for?' asked Belinda.

'I don't know,' said Holly. She stepped out on to the pavement. 'It feels wrong,' she said. 'Just leaving him like this.'

'We can't do anything,' said Tracy. 'Holly? Come on.'

'I want to make sure he's all right,' said Holly. She began to walk back along the quiet avenue.

Her two friends looked anxiously at each other, then followed her.

They were halfway to Mr Barnard's bungalow when they saw Tom Barnard come running down the path. He jumped into his car and sped off.

Holly ran forwards and hammered on the door of the bungalow. 'Mr Barnard?' she called. 'Are you all right?'

The door opened. Mr Barnard's face was white, but he didn't seem to be hurt.

'He's gone,' he told her. 'He won't be back. He's gone for good now. It's all over.'

16 Searching the school

Holly arrived at school the next morning with a curious feeling of anticlimax. After the revelations of the previous evening, it seemed strange just to be walking in to school as if nothing had happened.

Tom Barnard was gone. David was out of danger. The Mystery Club had phoned him from Holly's house the previous evening to tell him that Tom Barnard had left town. Everything seemed to have been resolved. But Holly couldn't shake the feeling that it wasn't quite over yet.

As soon as Tom Barnard had learned from his brother that his criminal intentions were known about, he had run to his car and had left Willow Dale. At least, that was what Mr Barnard had told them. Holly wasn't so sure.

Could it really be that easy?

Holly still felt that the police should have been informed. Was it enough simply to get rid of Tom Barnard? Shouldn't he be brought to justice?

Tracy came running up to her. 'Well?' she said, grinning. 'Are we brilliant detectives or what?' She noticed the frown on Holly's face. 'What's wrong?' she asked.

'Oh, nothing,' said Holly. 'I would have felt happier if the police had caught up with Tom Barnard, rather than Mr Barnard letting him get away like that. What if he comes back?'

'You heard what Mr Barnard said,' said Tracy. 'The guy's probably in Scotland by now and still running. We did it, Holly. We saved David all by ourselves. I think that's great, don't you?'

Holly smiled, caught up in her friend's good humour. 'I suppose so,' she said.

'And now,' said Tracy, 'we can finish off by finding the *White Lady*. Let's get Belinda and decide what we should do.' She looked up at the school building. 'I know you're in there, somewhere,' she called. 'And we're going to get you!'

Holly pulled herself out of her troubled thoughts. She looked round and saw Belinda ambling in through the school gates.

While they were chatting, they saw Miss Horswell's car come gliding into the teachers' car park.

'Let's tell her what we've found out,' said Tracy.

They ran up to her as she was getting out of her car.

'Miss Horswell! Can we speak to you?' asked Holly. 'It's really important.'

'Girls! Calm down,' said Miss Horswell. 'Let me get my breath.'

'We've discovered something else about the *White Lady*,' said Tracy.

'So soon?' said Miss Horswell. 'I'd imagined you'd be weeks going through the records.'

'We didn't find it there,' said Holly. 'It was pure luck, really.'

'Excuse me,' said Belinda. 'It wasn't *luck* at all.' She grinned at Miss Horswell. 'I spotted it.'

'Spotted what?' asked Miss Horswell.

'That the painting is somewhere in the school,' said Belinda.

Miss Horswell frowned at them. 'I don't think you can be right, there,' she said. 'You'd better come along to my office and tell me what you think you've discovered.'

Miss Horswell led them to her office and sat behind her desk as they told her what they had seen from the balloon.

She sat back, looking carefully at them. 'I've got to admit,' she said, 'sceptical as I am about this entire enterprise, it does look as if you might be on to something.'

'We could set up a major search,' said Tracy. 'Get everyone in the school involved. Like a huge treasure hunt.'

Miss Horswell eyed her with alarm. 'I don't like the sound of that, Tracy. Have you any idea how much chaos six hundred students could cause if they were let loose in the school? There wouldn't be one brick left standing by the time they'd finished.

164

If I am going to allow any sort of searching to go on, it will have to be done systematically and unobtrusively.' She rested her elbows on her desk and clasped her hands under her chin. 'I'm beginning to wonder, girls, whether it wouldn't be better to inform the governors at this stage. They might well think professional advice should be sought.'

'No!' said Holly. 'Don't do that, miss. Please.'

Miss Horswell continued. 'I was happy for you to do your investigating while I was certain the painting wouldn't be found, but . . .' She looked from girl to girl. 'I really think that the authorities should be contacted now that it seems there is a chance of it actually being discovered.'

'That's not fair, miss,' said Tracy. 'Not after we've done all the work. At least give us a chance.'

Miss Horswell smiled. 'I suppose you deserve that much,' she said. 'I'll tell you what. I'll make a compromise with you. You have my permission to conduct your own search during your free time today. In the meantime I shall speak to the school governors. What happens after that will be their decision.'

'One day?' said Tracy. 'Couldn't we have a bit longer than that?'

'I'm sorry,' said Miss Horswell. 'That's as much as I'm prepared to do for you.' She looked at their disappointed faces. 'Don't worry,' she said. 'If the governors show any interest in what I have to tell

165

them, I'll make sure you're kept fully informed of what they decide to do. Now, off you go.'

The three friends turned to leave.

'But remember,' said Miss Horswell. 'I don't want this turning into a free-for-all. Keep it to yourselves. And if you discover anything at all you're to come to me immediately. Is that understood?'

'Yes, miss,' said Holly.

They stood in the hall.

'It's always a mistake to involve teachers,' said Belinda, shaking her head. 'They can't bear to leave you alone.'

'One measly day,' said Tracy despondently. 'You couldn't search a place *half* this size in one day.'

'Not even a day, really,' said Holly. 'One lunch hour. I haven't got any free periods at all today.'

'I'm sure she'd let us carry on looking after school this afternoon,' said Belinda. 'That would give us a bit longer.'

'Big deal,' said Tracy. 'Another couple of hours.'

'It's better than nothing,' said Holly. 'I'll go and find Jamie. He can tell my mum and dad I'll be late home.' She smiled. 'Look on the bright side,' she said. 'At least it means Miss Horswell thinks there's a good chance the painting is going to turn up. Even if we don't find it ourselves, it'll still be us that worked out all the clues.'

They had hoped to be able to tell Samantha the news about David, and about the *White Lady*, but she still wasn't at school.

'I think we should find out how David is,' said Holly. 'I'm still not happy about that Tom Barnard.'

'He's gone,' said Tracy. 'David will be fine.'

'All the same,' said Holly. 'I think we should go and see him this evening.'

'Not until we've finished searching for the *White Lady*,' said Tracy. 'And when we find it we can tell him about that as well.' She grinned. 'He's going to think we're superhuman!'

At lunch-time the three girls met and planned their search.

'It's not the sort of thing that could be hidden in a drawer,' said Belinda. 'Even rolled up it's still going to be about a metre long. So we can assume it's not in any of the rooms that are used.'

They decided to start their hunt down in the basement area. They got the keys to all the old deserted rooms down there and spent their lunch hour getting dusty and dirty, but without any luck. All too soon the bell went for afternoon lessons.

'That gives us five minutes before school starts,' said Holly. 'We'd better get off to the washrooms.'

'We've got to find it now,' said Belinda, looking at herself in the washroom mirror. 'My mother will have me shot if I get home like this for no good reason.'

After school finished they met up again and prowled around the school grounds.

'Perhaps he buried it somewhere?' suggested Tracy. 'What were the words of that clue again?'

'"To find me, look behind me,"' said Belinda. She threw herself down in the grass. 'I'm exhausted,' she said. 'I think we should give up. I'm tired, I'm filthy, and I'm starved half to death. This is hopeless. What do you say we let the governors find it?'

Holly joined her friend in the grass. 'I'm beginning to think you're right,' she said. 'It's hopeless.'

Tracy stood over them, her hands on her hips. 'You quitters!' she said. '*I'm* not giving up.' She looked round at the school. 'Come on, you guys. One last look around back there?'

'Have a heart,' said Belinda. 'I'm whacked. You go and look, if you must. I've had enough.'

Tracy gave them a pitying look, then set off determinedly for the school building.

'I can see the headlines now,' she shouted back. '"Lost painting found by ace student detective Tracy Foster."'

'She's mad,' said Belinda, stretching out on her back. 'The headlines are more likely to read, "Student Tracy Foster collapses through over-work."'

Holly watched as Tracy went into the school. 'We ought to go with her,' she said. 'How about it, Belinda? One last go before the caretaker locks up for the night?'

Belinda blinked at her through her spectacles.

'Slave driver,' she said, heaving herself to her feet.

They made their way to the building.

As they walked along the corridor in search of their friend they heard the sound of running feet.

Holly looked round. 'Samantha!'

'Thank heavens,' gasped Samantha. 'I thought you might have gone. I've been looking everywhere for you.'

'I was told you weren't in today,' said Holly.

'I've been at the nursing home with my gran, who wasn't doing so well,' said Samantha. 'But she's a lot better now. I went to the Abbey to see David this afternoon. He's vanished, Holly. No one up there knows where he is. I phoned your house and your brother told me you were staying late at school. I've been searching the whole building. I thought David might have told you where he was going.'

'How long has he been missing?' asked Holly.

'They said he went off with a man this afternoon. I'm scared that something bad might be happening to him.'

'What man?' asked Belinda.

'I don't know. They just said it was a man in a grey car. But he didn't say where he was going.' She looked desperately at the two girls. 'We've got to do something.'

169

'Tom Barnard!' said Holly. 'I knew it. I knew he wouldn't just run away.'

'Mr Barnard?' said Samantha. 'What's he got to do with it?' Holly quickly explained the previous evening's discoveries.

'We've got to call the police,' said Holly. 'David could be in terrible danger.'

'We can phone from here,' said Belinda. 'There's a phone in the secretary's office.'

They ran to the front of the school, all thoughts of their search for the lost painting forgotten.

'Oh, no!' said Holly. The door to the office was locked.

'There's a phone booth outside,' said Belinda. 'We can call from there.'

They ran to the main doors. The teachers' car park was empty. It was well past home time. Even the special classes that went on after hours had packed up and gone.

'What about Tracy?' said Holly.

'She'll be all right,' said Belinda. 'The caretaker won't be locking up just yet. We'll come back for her after we've phoned.'

They were about to run down the steps when Holly shoved them back in through the doors.

'Look!' she gasped.

A grey car was parked by the gates. As they watched from their hiding-place, they saw three shadowy figures skirting the bushes that grew inside the school wall. After a few moments they began to move stealthily towards the building, looking around to check they weren't being observed.

'David!' cried Samantha.

'And Tom Barnard and Harry Owen,' said Belinda. 'Now what do we do?'

The three men walked quickly up to the driveway, Tom Barnard's hand gripping David's shoulder.

Holly backed into the shadows.

The three men were heading straight for the school. There was no way for the three girls to get out without being seen.

17 The final clue

'Keep out of sight!' said Holly, flattening herself behind the door. Tom Barnard, Harry Owen and David were heading straight for the building. She could hear their footsteps getting louder.

'Don't panic,' said Belinda. 'They didn't see us. Quick, we can get out the back way.'

Samantha was pressed against the wall, wide-eyed and shaking with fear. Holly grabbed her arm and pulled her along the wall in Belinda's wake.

They came to the corridor and ran.

The school had back entrances at the foot of each of the two flights of stairs that ran up the sides of the buildings. The girls crashed through the double doors that led to the stairwell and the way out.

'What about Tracy?' gasped Belinda. 'We can't just leave her in here.'

'She could be anywhere,' said Holly. 'We haven't got time to search for her.'

'I'm not going without her,' said Belinda. She looked up the stairs. 'You go. I'll catch up with you.'

'Belinda!' called Holly, but her friend was already dashing up the stairs.

Samantha tugged at Holly's sleeve. 'Come *on!*' she cried. 'We've got to get the police.' She ran down the short flight of stairs to the back entrance. As Holly raced after her she saw that Samantha was wrestling with the bar that held the door closed.

'It's locked!' exclaimed Samantha.

'It can't be,' said Holly. She wrenched at the unmoving bar. 'It was open five minutes ago.'

'The caretaker,' said Samantha. 'He's started locking up for the night.' She stared at Holly. 'We'll be trapped.'

'Not yet,' said Holly. 'There's still the other door.' They ran down the basement stairs and burst through the doors into the long, dark corridor that ran the length of the building.

Holly crept cautiously up the stairs to the ground floor, her ears straining for any sound of the three men. She beckoned for Samantha to follow.

It was no good. This door was locked as well. Holly ran to a window. She caught a glimpse of the caretaker wheeling his bike around to the front of the building. She didn't dare shout or hammer on the window. Any noise might bring Tom Barnard and Harry Owen down on them.

Samantha was saucer-eyed with panic.

Holly wrenched at the window.

'That's no use,' said Samantha. 'The windows are kept locked. What are we going to do?'

'They'll be in the building now,' said Holly. 'We might be able to slip out the front way.'

As she crept along the corridor that led to the front of the building, Holly could hear the blood pounding in her ears. At any second she feared that she would walk straight into the men.

'What are they doing here?' asked Samantha.

'I don't know,' whispered Holly. She came to the corner and slid a cautious eye out along the corridor that led to the entrance hall. The paintings stared down silently from the wood-panelled walls. The corridor was deserted.

'Come on,' whispered Holly.

Samantha stared at her. 'I can't!' she said. 'I'm scared.'

'You've got to,' said Holly. 'It's our only way out.' She caught hold of Samantha's wrist and pulled the frightened girl along behind her. Samantha tried to twist her arm out of Holly's grip.

'Let me go,' cried Samantha. 'We'll be caught.'

Holly paused. 'It's our only way of helping David,' she said. She looked into Samantha's eyes. 'It's our only chance of escaping.'

Samantha took a long, slow breath, swallowing her fear. She nodded.

As they approached the hall, Holly heard an ominous sound. The clank of a key turning in a lock and the rattle of someone checking that the door was secured. Holly let go of Samantha and ran for the doors.

They were closed. Unwittingly the caretaker had locked them in with the two dangerous men.

Holly crouched and flipped the letter-box open. In the oblong of light she could see the caretaker cycling away. He was already too far away to hear her, even if she shouted.

She stood up, her back to the doors.

'We're locked in,' she said, trying to sound calm. Her heart was beating like a hammer in her chest. 'We'll have to break a window.'

'No, wait,' said Samantha. 'I know where there's a phone. In the sick room.'

'Where's that?' asked Holly.

'Up on the first floor,' said Samantha.

'We'll have to risk it,' said Holly. 'We'll phone the police, then keep hidden until they arrive.'

The two girls tiptoed along the corridor to the stairs. The school was menacingly silent.

Holly heard a slight sound from upstairs. She stopped, trying to listen above the pounding of her own heartbeat.

There were glass panels in the doors that led to the corridor on the first floor. Holly crept to the doors and slowly raised her head. The corridor beyond the doors was empty. Perhaps she had imagined the noise.

She pushed the door open and beckoned for Samantha to follow.

A figure appeared at the far end of the corridor.

'Tracy!' shouted Samantha.

Tracy waved and walked towards them, obviously unaware of their danger.

As she passed the art room, the door opened and David stepped out. So that had been the sound Holly had heard. People going into the art room.

Tracy stared at him in amazement. 'David? What are – '

'Run!' shouted Holly. 'Tracy, run!'

But it was too late. Tom Barnard sprang out and caught hold of Tracy before she could move. He twisted his arm around her neck.

Samantha screamed.

'Get down here,' shouted Tom Barnard at the two girls. He tightened his grip on Tracy. 'Now!'

There was no choice. They couldn't run and leave Tracy in the hands of a man as ruthless as Tom Barnard.

Holly and Samantha walked towards the art room.

Harry Owen appeared in the doorway. 'You again,' he growled. 'You've got in the way once too often.'

'I'm sorry,' said David, his face ghost-white. 'I had to tell them. It was the only way I could save myself. I had to tell them about the *White Lady*. They won't hurt you. They just want the painting.'

Holly stared at him. Surely he must realise they didn't know exactly where the painting was?

Tom Barnard pushed the three girls into the art room. The copy of the *White Lady* was lying un-rolled on a table.

'Cut the chat,' said Tom Barnard. He released Tracy and sent her sprawling. He grabbed David's collar. 'Where is it?'

'I don't know,' said David. 'It's in here somewhere.' He looked desperately at Holly. 'Tell him, Holly.'

'You said you knew where it was,' said Harry Owen. 'You told us it was worth a fortune and you knew where it was hidden. If you've been lying to us . . .'

'It's here,' David said desperately. 'I don't know precisely where, but it's *here* somewhere.'

Tom Barnard twisted his hand in David's collar. 'I ought to just break your neck,' he said menacingly.

'He's telling the truth,' said Holly. 'We've collected all the clues. It's hidden in the school.' She decided on a final gamble to make some time for them. Belinda was still uncaptured. If she could stall the two men for a few minutes, maybe Belinda could escape and call for help.

'It's hidden in the basement,' said Holly. 'I'll show you.'

Tom Barnard glared at David. 'This painting had better be worth as much as you've said,' he snarled. His eyes turned to Holly. 'Take us there.'

Belinda's eyes rose above the glass panel in the door. She bit her lip, watching as Holly and her friends were led along the corridor.

She had managed to duck out of sight as the three men had come along to the art room. She had heard them talking about the painting. It hadn't taken her long to put two and two together. David had brought them here, hoping to find the painting and use it to bargain his way out of trouble. That much was obvious. What was less obvious to Belinda at that moment was what she could do to help.

She had found the doors locked. All the ground floor windows were secured. How was she to get out?

She crept to the head of the stairs. Everything looked so ordinary, so normal through the tall window. How long would it be before their parents began to worry about where they were? It could be hours. Anything could have happened by then.

She tried the window. It grated open several inches then jammed. She leaned out but there was no one visible to shout to. No way of getting a message to the outside world.

It was a long drop down to the tarmac. She glanced to one side. A sturdy drainpipe ran down the wall. Someone as fit and active as Tracy might be able to get down that way. Still, what other option did she have?

Belinda leaned further out and caught hold of the pipe.

She brought her knee up on to the sill, levering herself into the narrow gap of the half-open window. She breathed in and squeezed under the sash.

She suddenly found herself caught between the wooden jaws of the window. Her jacket had snagged. Her face crumpled in despair as she realised she couldn't move.

She wriggled and squirmed, all too aware of the yawning drop in front of her eyes. If she used too much force to free herself she might easily fall. But if she didn't get her jacket loose she'd be stuck there.

She let her breath out and fought back the dizziness that threatened to overwhelm her. She pulled back from the sill, and slid with a gasp to the floor inside the window.

Her escape attempt had failed.

The solemn, severe face of Winifred Bowen-Davies gazed down at the group gathered in the front hall.

Holly was counting on the fact that the two men didn't know the school. She could have led them straight down to the basement, but she planned on wasting a few precious minutes by taking them by as long a route as she could manage.

Tom Barnard snatched at Holly's arm, his fingers digging painfully into her. 'What are you playing at?' he rasped. 'Just how stupid do you think we are? Where do you think you're taking us?'

'Keep your temper,' said Harry Owen. 'We can get what we want without any violence.'

Tom Barnard gave him a narrow-eyed look. 'She's

179

got us running round in circles,' he said. 'Perhaps she needs to be taught a lesson.'

'No violence,' said Harry Owen. 'Let's just find that painting and get out of here.' He looked sharply at Holly. 'Don't mess us about, girl. Just lead us to that painting and you won't get hurt.'

'Don't make promises you can't keep,' said Tom Barnard with a harsh laugh. 'I still haven't decided what I'm going to do with them.'

Harry Owen looked nervously at him. 'We can tie them up,' he said. 'They won't be found until tomorrow. And by then we can both be well away from here.'

Tom Barnard smiled grimly. 'I'd rather not leave witnesses.'

Harry Owen's eyes widened, but he didn't say anything.

'Don't hurt the girls,' said David. 'You can do what you like with me, but don't hurt them.'

Tom Barnard sneered at him. 'It's a bit late for heroics,' he said. 'Whatever happens, you're coming with us.' He flicked his head towards Harry Owen. 'He might be stupid enough to believe you about this painting of yours, but I'm not letting you out of my sight until I'm sure it's worth as much as you've said it is. And if it isn't . . .' The rest of his threat hung heavily in the still air.

'You sure are a brave guy,' said Tracy. 'It must really make you feel great to know you can beat up a bunch of kids.'

'Don't!' said Samantha. 'Don't make them angry. Let them take the painting and go. Don't antagonise them.'

'Antagonise them?' said Tracy, looking at Tom Barnard. 'No, I wouldn't want to do that. Not big brave men like them.'

Tom Barnard released Holly's arm and made a move towards Tracy, his eyes blazing.

'Leave it,' said Harry Owen. He stood in front of Holly, his small, hard eyes boring into her face. 'Where's the painting? You're treading on thin ice, here. If you want to save yourself and your friends, you'd better get your act together.'

Holly felt her legs trembling. She couldn't look into his face. Behind his head the portrait of Winifred Bowen-Davies gazed sadly down at them.

Suddenly through her fear, something in the painting swam into focus. Holly's mouth fell open, her eyes widening.

Harry Owen looked sharply at her, then spun to look at the painting. 'What?' he said. 'Is this it?' He grabbed her by the shoulders and shook her. 'Is this the painting?'

'No,' said Holly. She pointed. 'But I've solved the final clue.'

All eyes turned to the tall painting of Winifred Bowen-Davies. Holly shook herself free of Harry Owen's grip and walked slowly towards it.

'It was here,' she said. 'It was here all along.'

18 The secret of the White Lady

'The *White Lady* is hidden behind here,' said Holly, pointing up at the portrait of Winifred Bowen-Davies.

Owen's eyes narrowed as he looked from Holly to the painting. 'You said it was in the basement,' he said.

Holly shook her head. 'I was wrong,' she said. 'It's here.'

Tom Barnard pushed Tracy towards her. 'Get it down,' he said. 'And if you're lying you're going to regret it.'

'I'm not lying,' said Holly. She looked at Tracy, who was staring anxiously at her. 'Help me,' said Holly. 'We'll need a couple of chairs.'

There was a row of chairs against the wall by the secretary's office. Holly and Tracy dragged two of them over to the portrait. They climbed on to them and took hold of either side of the gilt frame.

They lifted the painting up off its hooks. The chains rattled softly as it came free. Carefully they stepped down off the chairs, supporting the weight of the painting between them.

They lowered it face down on the floor. Around the inside of the back of the frame were a dozen or more wooden wedges that held the canvas in place.

They crouched and began to twist the wedges free.

'I hope you know what you're doing,' whispered Tracy to Holly.

Holly didn't say anything. She was hoping the same thing.

They lifted the back-board out of the frame. There, lying between the board and the canvas back of the painting of Winifred Bowen-Davies, was a second, smaller sheet of canvas.

Holly reached across and peeled the canvas back. A section of blue sky was revealed. Tracy helped her turn the canvas over.

The sad face of the White Lady looked up at them.

'Is that it?' said Owen.

'Yes,' breathed David. 'This is it. It must be.'

They stood up, looking down at the long lost painting.

Tom Barnard grinned. 'Roll it up,' he said.

Holly carefully rolled the canvas into a tube.

'Now,' said Owen, looking at Tom Barnard, 'let's tie these kids up and get out of here.'

'I'm not so sure,' said Tom Barnard darkly. 'They know who we are. I don't like the idea of leaving them to tell everything to the police.'

'We can't take them with us,' said Harry Owen. 'Listen, I told you, it's all fixed. If this painting is as valuable as the boy says, all we've got to do is take it to those people I told you about. We can be miles from here by morning. Let them tell the police what they like. It'll be too late by then.'

Tom Barnard gave Owen a fierce look. 'I trusted you before,' he said, 'and spent two years in prison.' His eyes raked over the three girls. 'It wouldn't take five minutes to shut them up for good.'

'You'll be spending a lot more than two years inside if you do something stupid now,' said Harry Owen. 'We can make sure they won't be found easily.' He smiled grimly. 'We'll put them somewhere where they won't be found for a good long time.'

Tom Barnard nodded. 'OK,' he said. 'Where?'

Harry Owen turned to look at Holly. 'Take us down to the basement,' he said.

The three girls were pushed into a storeroom in the basement. Harry Owen found some rope and Tom Barnard tied them tightly by the wrists and ankles.

'Think yourselves lucky,' he said as he closed the door on them, leaving them in the dark.

'David!' shouted Samantha.

The door slammed.

'I'll be all right,' they heard David shout as the two men took him away.

They listened to the retreating footsteps of the three men echoing along the corridor.

'Can either of you move at all?' asked Tracy, straining fruitlessly at the cords around her wrists.

No one bothered answering. Tom Barnard had done his job very thoroughly.

A dreadful silence descended.

'How did you know the painting was there?' asked Tracy.

Holly sighed. 'It was so obvious,' she said. 'I saw – '

'Shh!' said Samantha. 'Listen.'

In the silence they heard the sound of a stealthy movement outside the door.

They held their breath.

The door opened. They could see nothing in the darkness. The sudden flare of the light being switched on half-blinded them.

Belinda waved her hands for them to keep quiet. 'Don't breathe a word,' she mouthed. 'They're not far away yet.'

'Where have you been?' whispered Tracy.

'Keeping out of sight,' said Belinda, crouching to pick at the knots at Holly's wrists.

'They've got the painting,' whispered Holly. 'They're getting away.'

'Don't be so sure,' said Belinda. She unwound the rope from around Holly's wrists and started on the knots binding her ankles.

The two of them released Samantha and Tracy.

'We've got to get the police,' said Tracy. 'They've got some escape route planned. That Owen guy said they'd be miles away by the morning.'

'I don't think so,' said Belinda. 'Follow me.'

They crept after Belinda. At the foot of the stairs they paused. From the distance they heard a splintering sound.

The four girls glided silently up the stairs.

'All the doors are locked,' whispered Belinda. 'They'll have to break their way out.'

They came to a corner. Belinda held her arm out to halt them and glanced down the next corridor.

A window stood open. Harry Owen was clambering out. But even as Belinda watched, David made a desperate grab at Tom Barnard, throwing him back against the wall. Harry Owen turned at the noise, hanging half out of the window.

David made a break for it, but Tom Barnard's foot shot out and David sprawled headlong in the corridor.

'Right,' said Tom Barnard. 'You're going to pay for that.'

'We've got to help him!' shouted Belinda.

The four girls raced along the corridor as Tom Barnard brought his knee down on David's chest and raised his fist to strike.

Belinda crashed into him, dragging his arm back and throwing him off balance.

Tracy and Holly were only a split-second behind her. Using all her strength, Tracy hurled herself into the air and landed full-force on Tom Barnard's chest.

He let out a bellow of surprise and pain, floundering on the floor with Tracy on top of him.

Holly tried to pull David to his feet. Harry Owen was heaving himself back in through the window, a ferocious expression on his face.

Tom Barnard gave a heave that sent Tracy flying, and his hand caught Belinda's ankle.

Belinda tripped and fell forwards, her head hitting Harry Owen in the stomach. He gave a gasp, clutching at her as he fell backwards through the window. There was a thud as he landed heavily on the grass.

Tom Barnard dragged himself to his feet. The girls backed away from him.

Suddenly there were other noises from outside.

Belinda hung out of the window. 'Over here! Over here!' she shouted.

Tom Barnard spun round. Through the open window they could see policemen running across the grass.

David ran forwards, catching Tom Barnard in the instant that his attention was diverted. But David wasn't strong enough to hold Tom Barnard. An elbow lashed back and David reeled away, his hands to his face.

From her sprawl on the floor, Tracy kicked

out, catching Tom Barnard's shin as Holly and Samantha pushed him.

He fell across the windowsill and Belinda brought the sash hammering down across his back.

Strong arms grabbed at him from outside. His feet flailed for a moment as the policemen dragged him out and pinned him down on the grass.

'Way to go, Belinda!' yelled Tracy, hauling up the window sash and springing down on to the grass.

The others leaned out of the window.

There were four policemen holding Tom Barnard down, and another two standing over Harry Owen.

David and the three girls climbed out of the window as the policemen dragged Harry Owen and Tom Barnard to their feet.

'Which of you is Belinda Hayes?' asked an officer. 'The girl who phoned?'

'That's me,' said Belinda with a grin. She looked at the others. 'I remembered there was a phone in the sick room. I phoned from there while you were keeping them occupied.' She smiled at the policeman. 'I'm glad you got here so quickly,' she said.

'We do our best,' said the policeman. He looked at the four girls. 'Anyone hurt?' he asked.

'No,' said Holly, grinning. 'We're fine.' She looked round at David. His lip was cut. 'Aren't we?'

He nodded. 'Yes,' he said. 'We're all fine, thanks to Belinda.'

'And me,' said Tracy. 'Did you see that flying tackle?'

'I think I've wrenched my ankle,' said Belinda. 'When he grabbed me.' She hopped over to lean on Holly.

Holly picked up the rolled canvas which had fallen out of Harry Owen's hands when he had fallen.

'So?' said the policeman. 'What's been going on here, then?'

It was the morning after all the excitement. The portrait of Winifred Bowen-Davies was back in its place on the wall. Holly, standing under it, was the centre of attention.

Miss Horswell was there. And Mr Barnard, Samantha and Belinda and Tracy.

'It all fell into place yesterday evening,' said Holly. She looked at her two friends. 'Remember I said I was sure I'd seen that magpie brooch somewhere before?' She pointed up at the painting. There, on Winifred Bowen-Davies's bodice, lay a shadowy black and white shape. The shape of a bird.

'It was here all along,' said Holly. 'But the painting is so dark that I hardly recognised it. It's the exact twin of the brooch that Roderick painted on his version of the White Lady. And it was Samantha who told me that the brooch her grandmother lent her was one of a pair. It

189

fitted in with the two other clues. The plan was of the school, you see. Belinda spotted that. And the words on the summer-house said "To find me, look behind me." But it didn't mean look inside the summer-house. It meant look behind the picture with the magpie brooch on it. The White Lady gave Hugo one of the pair of brooches when she left the Abbey. But she must have kept the other one.' Holly grinned. 'And that proves something else as well.' She picked up the canvas and held the *White Lady* out in front of her. 'Can you see?'

They looked at the painting.

'Good heavens,' said Miss Horswell, her hand to her mouth. 'I *do* see.'

'It's the eyes,' said Holly. 'The same sad eyes.'

'Winifred Bowen-Davies was the White Lady,' said Mr Barnard.

'That's right,' said Holly. 'She must have been very young when she posed for the *White Lady* portrait.'

'And she was in her eighties when our portrait of her was done,' said Miss Horswell. 'The face is quite different, until you look carefully. But you're right, Holly, they're both of the same woman. They're both Winifred Bowen-Davies.'

'So that's what she did after she left Woodfree Abbey,' said Mr Barnard. 'She set up this school. And that was why Hugo Bastable gave the school such a valuable painting as a nest egg. After he'd stolen it, Roderick must have hidden the painting here, intending to come back for it after the police had searched the Abbey. But he wound up in prison before he could get back here.'

'You've all done marvellously,' said Miss Horswell. 'You don't realise how very much this means to the school, girls. I have already spoken to the governors. We have decided to sell the painting.' She smiled. 'We don't want to risk it vanishing a second time. With the money we shall raise from the sale we'll be able to build that new gymnasium.'

'A new gym?' said Belinda. 'Couldn't you build something a bit more useful? Like a brand new canteen? Now *that* would make all the effort worthwhile.'

They all laughed.

Belinda looked at them, affronted. 'Or a stable?' she suggested. 'Then we could buy some horses, and . . . I don't know what everyone's finding so funny.' She turned and, with all the dignity she could muster, limped on her bandaged foot over to one of the chairs and sat down.

'Well,' she muttered. 'I'm glad everyone else is enjoying themselves. After everything I've been through. Falling through rotten ceilings, being hijacked in a hot air balloon, risking my neck out of windows, phoning the police and ending up with some maniac nearly pulling my foot off. You'd think I would get *something* worthwhile out of it.'

'I'll see what I can do for you,' said Miss Horswell. 'Meanwhile, I think it's time we were all getting off to our lessons.' She smiled at Holly. 'I hope you'll be writing a piece for the school magazine about this, Holly.'

'I most certainly will,' said Holly.

Miss Horswell went into her office.

Mr Barnard stood looking thoughtfully at the painting of Winifred Bowen-Davies.

'What will happen to your brother?' Tracy asked him.

Mr Barnard shook his head. 'He'll go back to prison, I expect. And Harry Owen along with him.' He smiled at Samantha. 'At least your friend David is out of trouble.'

He looked at the three friends. 'You've taught me a lesson,' he said. 'I should have done something about Tom as soon as he appeared. If I hadn't been so worried about my reputation you wouldn't have been put in all that danger.'

'It wasn't your fault,' said Holly. 'You didn't know what he was up to.'

Mr Barnard sighed. 'I should have guessed,' he said. 'Tom has always been wrong-headed.' He smiled wanly. 'Still, he's going to be paying for it now.'

They watched as he walked slowly away.

'I've just got one more thing to do,' said Holly. 'I'll see you later.'

She made her way over to the school library.

Steffie Smith was sitting behind her table, her chin in her hands, staring blankly at the visual display unit of her word processor.

'I've written something for the magazine,' said Holly.

Steffie looked up at her. 'Oh, yes?' she said. 'I suppose it's a twenty-page report of how you found that painting, is it?'

'No,' said Holly. 'Not twenty pages.' She laid a single sheet of paper on the desk. 'I think you'll like it,' she said.

Steffie glanced at it. 'We'll see,' she said.

'Miss Horswell said it should go in,' said Holly firmly.

'I know she did,' said Steffie. 'She told me. And I'm supposed to put it in exactly as you've written it.' She picked the sheet of paper up and dropped it in her "In" tray. 'Don't worry,' she said. 'I won't alter a word – no matter how much I don't like it.'

With a quiet smile, Holly left her to it.

Tracy and Belinda were waiting for her in the hall. Kurt was there as well, with his camera.

'I thought you might like me to take a group portrait,' he said. 'For the *Express*. You're going to be famous.'

'What did I tell you?' said Tracy. 'It'll be headline news. "Student detectives find missing painting"!'

Holly grinned. It seemed as if their wildest dreams were coming true.

They posed for a photograph under the painting of Winifred Bowen-Davies.

After Kurt had gone they stood looking up at the portrait of the school's founder.

'Steffie's not too pleased about all this,' said Holly. 'I've just given her my report about the painting.'

'Without showing us first?' said Tracy. 'I hope you've remembered to mention everything I did.'

'Everything *you* did?' said Belinda. 'I like that. Who was it that stopped those crooks getting away with the *White Lady* in the end?'

'Hold on a minute,' said Holly. 'Who was it that solved the last clue? It would never have been found at all without me.'

'If I hadn't carried on searching after you two had given up, we wouldn't even have *been* in the school,' said Tracy.

'But I found out it was in the school in the first place,' said Belinda. 'I should get star billing.' She looked at Holly. 'Well?' she said. 'Who *did* get star billing in your report?'

Holly smiled. 'The Mystery Club,' she said.

Her two friends looked at her and laughed.

'Anyone for ice cream at lunch-time?' said Belinda. 'To celebrate solving our first mystery.'

'Our first mystery,' said Holly with a smile. 'And this is just the start. Who knows what might be coming next?'

DOUBLE DANGER

by Fiona Kelly

Holly, Belinda and Tracy are back in the second thrilling adventure in the Mystery Club series, published by Knight Books.

Here is the first chapter . . .

1 Eighty miles an hour

It was chaos at home as usual, so Holly Adams took off on her bike. Happy holiday! No school, no hassle, not even any Mystery Club meetings. Just a bike ride over the moor on a peaceful sunny day. She let go of the brakes on a downhill stretch, hair flying free, feeling the warmth on her face.

Trouble was the last thing Holly Adams wanted today, but like iron filings to a magnet, it found her. Out here, riding free along the ridge of the moorside, with Willow Dale spread out like an *A to Z* below, a black bullet shape roared past her at eighty miles an hour. It came and was gone in a hot, mean rush.

'Idiot!' Holly wobbled and fell sideways into bilberry bushes. Sitting there, she swore loudly. The driver was a tanned man in dark glasses and a white open-necked shirt. She'd caught sight of him leering sideways at her as he forced her off the road.

Gingerly, Holly stood up. 'Oh, no!' she groaned. Blue juice from the berries had stained her T-shirt, and her front wheel had lost a couple of spokes.

She got back on her bike, shaky and angry. As she wobbled along again, Holly planned an article for Steffie Smith, editor of *Winformation*, the school magazine: 'Cyclists Call for Safety. End of the Road for Lunatic Motorists!'

But her plan for revenge soon went smash. She rounded a bend, saw the black car swoop into the dip and take the next hill with a throaty roar. She heard the brakes, saw it leave the road, rear up over the banking and tear through a dry-stone wall.

With fear gripping her throat, Holly took the descent and pedalled like mad up the next hill, in time to see the car still lurching over rough purple heather. By now it was out of control. It hit a rock on the skyline with a sickening crunch and slewed sideways. Spinning like a toy, it disappeared over the edge.

Holly felt her heart flip. She dropped her bike and ran towards the outcrop of rocks. The heather pulled and tripped her, but she staggered on. A worker raced out of a nearby barn, running with Holly towards the noise. They reached the crag together. The man caught Holly's arm. 'Stop!' he yelled.

She looked down. There was a sheer edge. The rock fell into nothing. Steadying themselves, the man and Holly peered down at the car fifty feet below. It was turned on its back like a helpless beetle, wheels still spinning. The man breathed in sharply. Holly held on to him. What she noticed, after the screeching brakes, the scraping metal, the crunching, the sliding and the smashing, was the complete silence. A curlew rose from the heather and soared overhead.

'Stay here!' the man said to Holly. He started to scramble diagonally down the cliff, using a sheep track. He grabbed clumps of coarse grass and found footholds on the steep slope. Below, the wheels of the car still spun in the eerie silence.

No way am I stopping here, Holly thought. She set off after him. Less strong, but more agile, she soon caught him up. They reached the bottom together.

'Steady on.' The farm worker gasped for breath. 'It's dangerous. We should go back . . . Get help.' They looked at the battered shell of the car, its windows blank and crazed, its tyres spinning gently.

'No!' Holly thought of the driver. 'He needs help now. Let's go.' She tugged at the man's sleeve, pulling him forward through the long grass.

'The whole thing could go up in flames,' the man warned.

Holly nodded, but she knew they'd have to take the risk.

The slow click-click-click of the turning wheels broke the silence. They were near enough to try the driver's door.

Jammed. The shell was so buckled out of shape that none of the doors would open. Frantically they pulled. The driver was in there injured; unconscious or worse.

The man pushed Holly back. They were sweating and scratched from the brambles. 'It's no use. We need help.'

Holly nodded this time and gasped out, 'Go and ring the police. I'll stay.' She squatted by the smashed car, her nerves steadying, determined to wait.

The man glanced once at her stubborn face, then nodded and ran off. He scrambled up the ledge, out of sight.

The sun beat down and the place smelt of petrol and smouldering tyres. It could all go up in flames, like the man said. The stupid wheels turned on. *I have to do something*, Holly thought.

She had to try to open the bashed metal cage. She just wanted to let the driver see someone was here to help. But trying to see through the crazy pattern of splintered safety glass was impossible.

Holly thought at the speed of light. True, she couldn't open a door, but she could push through a shattered window and gain access that way. There were stones, hand-sized stones, everywhere. Holly grasped one, chose the passenger side window, took a deep breath and hammered. The dull thud of disintegrating safety glass sounded sinister. Holly drew breath. She chipped away at the glass until she could peer inside.

It was dark. The petrol smell made her sick and

faint. Or was it dread? She looked for a body, pale faced, twisted; maybe bloody, maybe dreadfully disfigured. But nothing moved. There was nothing in the driver's seat, nothing on the floor, or flung by the impact into the back seat. There was nothing at all in the car.

Holly pulled her face out of the darkness into sunlight. 'Nothing!' She gave a hollow laugh. It wasn't funny. *Make sure*, she told herself. It defied common sense.

She looked again, but there was still no one in the car. It didn't just crash itself. Locked in her memory was the man in dark glasses speeding down the road.

Horror crept back in.

Suppose he was thrown out. Suppose a door was flung open as the car hit the cliff edge. There would be a body somewhere on the cliff, or down here in what looked now like a disused quarry, with sheer sides all around, and boulders littering the bottom. *There'll be a body*, Holly told herself over and over. She squatted at a safe distance and began to shiver in the midday sun.

Suddenly the day was ripped apart by a boom of metal and a roar of flames. The car exploded. Holly flattened herself behind a boulder. Bits of glass and metal flew in all directions and black smoke billowed overhead in a mushroom cloud as flames enveloped the wreck.

The farm worker came running back with his

father. 'Luke, you see if the girl's OK!' the older man yelled.

'You OK?' he asked Holly. She nodded.

The police cars and Land Rovers roared to the scene within minutes. The cliff top swarmed with uniforms. Firemen's hoses snaked down into the quarry, and men with radio phones and huge steel claws and winding gear to prise the car open.

Holly watched the men douse the flames. 'There's no one in there,' she told them. 'It's empty.'

A fireman gave her a stern look and went on with the job.

'I looked,' Holly told Luke. 'I broke a window. There's no one in there.'

Luke shook his head, watching intently.

'Get the girl out of here,' a man in uniform ordered. He clearly thought Holly couldn't take the strain.

'No, I'm OK,' Holly protested. She'd seen it through this far, hadn't she?

'He's right,' Luke said quietly. 'There's no need for us to stick around any longer.' He took Holly by the hand.

'Maybe the driver got thrown out. He's probably lying injured!' she protested again.

'That's their business, not ours,' he told her. 'We've done our bit.' He was gentle, but he led her firmly from the scene of the accident, back up the cliff to his house, where his mother gave Holly endless cups of tea, and they waited.

The police found nothing. They searched the burnt-out wreck, the quarry, the cliff and the scarred heather. They came to the farmhouse with the news; the driver was nowhere to be found.

Back home at Holly's cottage, it all came out on the evening news: 'Driver missing after moor top crash.' The police were appealing for further witnesses.

A reporter from the *Willow Dale Express* rang, wanting to interview Holly, but her mother refused. 'No, I'm sorry she's much too tired,' Mrs Adams said in her brisk, bank manager voice. She put the phone down firmly.

'Thanks, Mum!' Holly pulled a face. 'Are you a spoilsport, or what?'

'No. I'm a sensible mum who knows best!' Mrs Adams said. 'Newspapers always get hold of things and twist them about. Anyway, you are tired.'

'After my ordeal?' But Holly knew when to give in. She smiled, despite her disappointment. 'Can I just ring Tracy and Belinda?' she pleaded. The whole town had heard about the mysterious accident, but no one knew that she, Holly Adams, was the chief witness. Did she have a story to tell the Mystery Club!

'How many times have I heard those words!'

her mother said with a laugh. She paused, then relented. 'I suppose . . .'

Holly gave her a grin and a hug, then made a grab for the phone.

'Wow! I'll be right there!' Tracy squealed, as soon as Holly told her the news. 'Wow!' She slammed down the receiver.

'I'll get my mum to drive me right down,' Belinda said. 'And don't tell dare you Tracy a single word until I get there!'

They arrived together, Tracy with her short blonde hair, grinning with excitement. Belinda, slower, heavier, but with her usual eye for mystery. Tracy was breathless and wanted to know everything all at once so she could figure it out first. Belinda took it in slowly, turned it over, and frowned through her wire-rimmed glasses. Together again, the Mystery Club.

Mrs Adams brought three hot chocolates up to Holly's room. The three girls were sitting in a triangle on Holly's bed.

'Don't tire her out!' Mrs Adams warned as she shut the door on them.

'We won't!' they chorused, ignoring her of course.

'So?' Belinda demanded, leaning forward.

'So what?' Holly was enjoying their suspense.

'So a guy can't vanish into thin air!' cried Tracy.

'Well, I hate to say it, but I think we've got

another mystery on our hands!' Holly said. She smiled.

'Let's go up there tomorrow and search for clues!' Tracy suggested, all action as usual.

They agreed; it should be their first move.

'The police and fire engine moved the car,' Holly said. 'But there are skid marks, the broken wall, all of that for us to look at.'

Belinda sat quietly for a moment. 'Was the car a write-off?' she asked finally, fiddling with the frayed hem of her jeans. 'A total write-off?'

Holly nodded. 'I'll say. It blew up into a million pieces!'

'Do you have any idea of how much a car like that is worth?' said Belinda. She paused for effect. 'I asked my dad when it came up on the news.'

'How much?' Tracy and Holly asked together.

'Thirty-five grand!'

Silence showed their astonishment.

'That's an awful lot of car!' Tracy said at last, half whistling.

'So?' Holly said. 'Am I thinking what you're thinking?'

'What am I thinking?' Tracy asked.

'You're thinking what Belinda was thinking when she told us about the thirty-five grand, right?' Holly's voice was a whisper now.

Their three heads leaned together. 'A set-up!' they cried.

'That's right,' declared Holly. 'A staged accident

for thirty-five thousand pounds' worth of insurance money!'

'Prove it!' Jamie, Holly's little brother and professional pest, burst open the door.

Holly chucked a pillow at him. 'Scram! You know you're not supposed to listen at keyholes!'

'Prove it! Prove it!' Jamie jeered, dodging the pillow.

'Go boil your head, Jamie!' Tracy scowled.

But Belinda only blinked at him over her glasses. 'Oh, we will,' she told him. 'We most certainly will!'

THE MYSTERY CLUB

The Mystery Club members Holly, Tracy and Belinda love
adventure and suspense. What better way to follow their
exploits than to wear their specially designed T-shirt and
record all your secrets in the Mystery Club notebook
with a Mystery Club pen? Whilst reading their latest
adventure you can make sure you're not dicturbed with
the unique door hanger. And don't lose your place
with the Mystery Club bookmark.

TO OBTAIN YOUR KIT ALL YOU HAVE TO DO IS:-

1   Fill out the form below with your name, address and the number of kits
    you require.
2   Make out a postal order or cheque to Hodder & Stoughton Ltd for £4.99
    per kit or fill in the credit card details on the form.
3   Send the form with your payment to The Mystery Club Room, 47
    Bedford Square, London WC1B 3DP.

- -

Don't Miss Out – Be A Part Of The Action!

Sorry, only available to UK addresses until 31 December 1994.
Allow 28 days for delivery. Available only while stocks last.

No. of kits required at £4.99 each . . . .

Cheque or postal order enclosed to the value of £ . . . . OR

Card Number . . . .

Amount . . . . Expiry Date . . . .

Signed . . . .

Cardholder's name and address (if different from below)

Name . . . .

Address . . . .

. . . . Postcode . . . .

PLEASE SEND MY KIT(S) TO (please print your name and address clearly)

Name . . . .

Address . . . .

. . . . Postcode . . . .

ISBN 0 340 60455 7